THE BILLIONAIRE'S IMPROMPTU BET

A SWEET BILLIONAIRES SECOND CHANCE ROMANCE

LORANA HOOPES

For my Family who lets me write.

To Jesse K. Thanks for being the inspiration for the Jesse in my book. Hope you love the new cover.

This book was originally titled Lawfully Pursed, but I think this title fits it better.

❀ Created with Vellum

NOTE FROM THE AUTHOR

Thank you so much for picking up this book. I hope you enjoy the story and the characters as they are dear to my heart. If you do, please leave a review at your retailer. It really does make a difference because it lets people make an informed decision about books. Below are the other books in this series. I would love for you to check them out. I'd also like to offer you a sample of my newest book. Free Sample!

Sign up for Lorana Hoopes's VIP newsletter and get her short story, The Reality Bride's Baby, as a welcome gift. Get Started Now!

The rest of the Sweet Billionaire series:

The Billionaire's Secret

A Brush with a Billionaire

The Billionaire's Christmas Miracle

The Billionaire's Cowboy Groom

The Cowboy Billionaire coming soon!

1

Brie Carter fell back spread eagle on her queen-sized canopy bed sending her blond hair fanning out behind her. With a large sigh, she uttered, "I'm bored."

"How can you be bored? You have like millions of dollars." Her friend, Ariel, plopped down in a seated position on the bed beside her and flicked her raven hair off her shoulder. "You want to go shopping? I hear Tiffany's is having a special right now."

Brie rolled her eyes. Shopping? Where was the excitement in that? With her three platinum cards, she could go shopping whenever she wanted. "No, I'm bored with shopping too. I have everything. I want to do something exciting. Something we don't normally do."

Brie enjoyed being rich. She loved the unlimited credit cards at her disposal, the constant apparel of new clothes, and of course the penthouse apartment her father paid for, but lately, she longed for something more fulfilling.

Ariel's hazel eyes widened. "I know. There's a new bar down on Franklin Street. Why don't we go play a little game?"

Brie sat up, intrigued at the secrecy and the twinkle in Ariel's eyes. "What kind of game?"

"A betting game. You let me pick out any man in the place. Then you try to get him to propose to you."

Brie wrinkled her nose. "But I don't want to get married." She loved her freedom and didn't want to share her penthouse with anyone, especially some man.

"You don't marry him, silly. You just get him to propose."

Brie bit her lip as she thought. It had been awhile since her last relationship and having a man dote on her for a month might be interesting, but…. "I don't know. It doesn't seem very nice."

"How about I sweeten the pot? If you win, I'll set you up on a date with my brother."

Brie cocked her head. Was she serious? The only thing Brie couldn't seem to buy in the world was the affection of Ariel's very handsome, very wealthy, brother. He was a movie star, just the kind of person Brie could consider marrying in the future. She'd had a crush on him as long as she and Ariel had been friends, but he'd always seen her as just that, his little sister's friend. "I thought you didn't want me dating your brother."

"I don't." Ariel shrugged. "But he's between girlfriends right now, and I know you've wanted it for ages. If you win this bet, I'll set you up. I can't guarantee any more than one date though. The rest will be up to you."

Brie wasn't worried about that. Charm she possessed in abundance. She simply needed some alone time with him, and she was certain she'd be able to convince him they were meant to be together. "All right. You've got a deal."

Ariel smiled. "Perfect. Let's get you changed then and see who the lucky man will be.

A tiny tug pulled on Brie's heart that this still wasn't right, but she dismissed it. This was simply a means to an end, and he'd never have to know.

Jesse Calhoun relaxed as the rhythmic thudding of the speed bag reached his ears. Though he loved his job, it was stressful being the SWAT sniper. He hated having to take human lives and today had been especially rough. The team had been called out to a drug bust, and Jesse was forced to return fire at three hostiles. He didn't care that they fired at his team and himself first. Taking a life was always hard, and every one of them haunted his dreams.

"You gonna bust that one too?" His co-worker Brendan appeared by his side. Brendan was the opposite of Jesse in nearly every way. Where Jesse's hair was a dark copper, Brendan's was nearly black. Jesse sported paler skin and a dusting of freckles across his nose, but Brendan's skin was naturally dark and freckle free.

Jesse flashed a crooked grin, but kept his eyes on the small, swinging black bag. The speed bag was his way to release, but a few times he had started hitting while still too keyed up and he had ruptured the bag. Okay, five times, but who was counting really? Besides, it was a better way to calm his nerves than other things he could choose. Drinking, fights, gambling, women.

"Nah, I think this one will last a little longer." His shoulders began to burn, and he gave the bag another few punches for good measure before dropping his arms and letting it swing to a stop. "See? It lives to be hit at least another day." Every once in a while, Jesse missed training the way he used to. Before he joined the force, he had been an amateur boxer, on his way to being a pro, but a shoulder injury had delayed his training and forced him to consider something else. It had eventually healed, but by then he had lost his edge.

"Hey, why don't you come drink with us?" Brendan clapped a hand on Jesse's shoulder as they headed into the locker room.

"You know I don't drink." Jesse often felt like the outsider of the team. While half of the six-man team was married, the other half found solace in empty bottles and meaningless relationships. Jesse understood that - their job was such that they never knew if they would come home night after night - but he still couldn't partake.

Brendan opened his locker and pulled out a clean shirt. He peeled off his current one and added deodorant before tugging on the new one. "You don't have to drink. Look, I won't drink either. Just come and hang out with us. You have no one waiting for you at home."

That wasn't entirely true. Jesse had Bugsy, his Boston Terrier, but he understood Brendan's point. Most days, Jesse went home, fed Bugsy, made dinner, and fell asleep watching TV on the couch. It wasn't much of a life. "All right, I'll go, but I'm not drinking."

Brendan's lips pulled back to reveal his perfectly white teeth. He bragged about them, but Jesse knew they were veneers. "That's the spirit. Hurry up and change. We don't want to leave the rest of the team waiting."

"Is everyone coming?" Jesse pulled out his shower necessities. Brendan might feel comfortable going out with just a new application of deodorant, but Jesse needed to wash more than just dirt and sweat off. He needed to wash the sound of the bullets and the sight of lifeless bodies from his mind.

"Yeah, Pat's wife is pregnant again and demanding some crazy food concoctions. Pat agreed to pick them up if she let him have an hour. Cam and Jared's wives are having a girls' night, so the whole gang can be together. It will be nice to hang out when we aren't worried about being shot at."

"Fine. Give me ten minutes. Unlike you, I like to clean up before I go out."

Brendan smirked. "I've never had any complaints. Besides, do you know how long it takes me to get my hair like this?"

Jesse shook his head as he walked into the shower, but he knew it was true. Brendan had rugged good looks and muscles to match. He rarely had a hard time finding a woman. Jesse on the other hand hadn't dated anyone in the last few months. It wasn't that he hadn't been looking, but he was quieter than his teammates. And he wasn't looking for right now. He was looking for forever. He just hadn't found it yet.

2

A nervous feeling blanketed Brie as they entered the bar. Who would Ariel choose? Hopefully, someone handsome. Brie was a good actress, but not that good. She could never convince someone she cared about them if she didn't at least find them attractive.

"Let's get a drink while we scan your options," Ariel said as she flicked her dark hair over her shoulder and sashayed up to the bar. "Hi," - she leaned seductively on the counter - "Can I get two strawberry lemonade vodkas?"

"Sure thing, doll." The bartender flashed her a wink and a sly grin before turning to make their drinks.

While they waited, Brie scanned the crowd. It appeared to be one of the hipper places in New York, and she was pleased to see many good-looking men. Maybe this wouldn't be so bad after all.

"Here you go, doll." The bartender's voice grabbed Brie's attention and she turned back to where Ariel was shamelessly flirting with the bartender.

"Thank you, how much do I owe you?" She batted her eyes and moved as if she were going to reach for her purse, but the bartender stayed her arm.

"First one's on me. I can't have beautiful women going thirsty on me."

Ariel flashed a wink at the handsome man and grabbed the drinks. Then she led the way to an empty table. "Now, let's see who looks like a good match for you."

As her eyes roved over the men in the room, Brie's nerves knotted again. What if it were someone awful, someone completely incompatible with her?

"There." Ariel smiled as she pointed discreetly at a table where six men sat talking and laughing.

"Which one?" Brie was relieved to see all of them were nice looking, but she had her eye on the olive skinned dark-haired one. He looked fun and mysterious.

Ariel's lips pursed, and her eyes narrowed as she studied the men. "That one. The one with the copper colored hair." Her lips pulled into a smile Brie would have sworn was malicious if she weren't her best friend.

Brie shifted her attention from the Greek god to the man next to him, and her heart sank. Though handsome, he sat straight and didn't seem nearly as easy going as the rest of the men at the table. In fact, the drink in front of him was clear, so unless it was straight vodka, Brie was fairly certain he was drinking water. "Him? Why?"

"Why not? He looks wholesome and like he could use a good woman."

Brie rolled her eyes. Wholesome was a quality she associated with food, not men. "How am I even supposed to talk to him? He has five friends with him."

"Well, I happen to know one of them is a police officer, so it's a good chance the rest are too. Go buy them a round and thank them for serving us and then cozy up to him."

"Your brother better be worth it," Brie hissed under her breath. This was way out of her comfort zone.

She smoothed her skirt as she stood and made her way to the bar. "Can I get six beers for that group right there?" She pointed to the table where her target sat.

"Sure thing. That will be sixty dollars."

Brie handed over her credit card, signed the slip, and then waited until the beers were ready. She followed the server over to the table and put on her best smile.

"Someone told me New York's finest were sitting here. I wanted to say thank you for keeping us safe by offering you a round."

"Well, we appreciate that," the dark-haired one she had been eying said. "Why don't you join us for a drink?"

"Don't mind if I do." Brie grabbed an empty chair and scooted into the space between her target and the one she wished were her target. "I'm Brie Carter by the way."

"Brendan Decker." The dark-haired one stuck out his hand. "Wait, Brie Carter. Like the daughter to Phil Carter, the investment billionaire?"

"Yep, that's me." She turned her attention to her target who had not touched his beer and didn't seem to be paying attention to her and Brendan at all. "You don't drink?"

He turned his hazel eyes on her. "Not a drop, but I'm sure one of my friends will happily drink this one."

"Come on, Jesse, it's rude to refuse such a kind gesture from such a beautiful woman," Brendan said.

"No, it's fine." Brie smiled at Jesse. "I don't want him to drink it if he doesn't want to." Oh, how Brie wished Brendan were her target. He seemed like he wanted to carry on a conversation with her while Jesse seemed content to scan the crowd and check his watch.

"Okay, well, let me introduce you to everyone," Brendan said, placing a hand on her arm to get her attention again. "You've met the stoic Jesse Calhoun there. He's the sharpshooter of the group. Amazingly steady hands on that one and nerves of steel. Then we have the team leader Patrick Hughes there." He pointed to the oldest man at the table, an average looking man with a head of brown hair that was graying at the temples. "Don't let his age fool you, he's still tough as nails.

Course he has to be with five kids and another one on the way."

Brie's eyes widened in surprise. "Oh, my goodness. Well, congratulations?"

Brendan chuckled and continued his introductions. "Next to him is the muscle, Cam Crawford. I'm not sure how he's still married since he spends his free time pumping iron in the gym."

"She loves it," Cam said with a smile and a twinkle in his green eyes.

"I'll bet she does. Then we have Jared Malone, the tactical brains of the operation."

Brie smiled at the studious looking Jared. A pair of glasses sat on the bridge of his nose, but she could clearly see his kind brown eyes.

"Last but not least is the daredevil of the group. That's Carter Douglas. We don't let him drive because he likes to speed too much."

The blond Carter Douglas flashed her a hand wave, and Brie could almost sense the danger emanating from him.

"Nice to meet you all. Are you an elite group?"

Brendan puffed out his chest. "You're looking at one of the best SWAT teams in the city."

"Hey, man, I'm gonna bug out of here." Jesse leaned around Brie as if she didn't exist as he addressed Brendan.

"Me too." Patrick finished the beer he was drinking

and set it back on the table. "I have to go get pickles and ice cream." He rolled his eyes and shook his head.

"Yeah, we should go too," Cam said to Jared. "The girls should be home soon." Jared nodded and finished the last of his drink as well.

"Well, it was nice to meet you all." Brie wasn't ready to leave, but she didn't know how to stay without looking desperate and she certainly had no idea how to follow Jesse.

"Stay." Brendan placed a hand on her arm. "I'd love to get to know you better."

"Oh, I," Brie looked to Jesse, but he was paying no attention to her, "All right." Maybe she could glean some information about how to reach Jesse from his friend. "Would you mind if I bring my friend, Ariel, over?"

Brendan shrugged. "Looks like we'll have plenty of room."

"Great, I'll be right back." Brie crossed the small room back to her table where Ariel was waiting.

"What are you doing? You let the one you're supposed to be with get away."

Brie shot her a look. "Yeah, well you picked the toughest case. He wasn't interested in me or any conversation. So, now I must try Plan B. I'm going to see if I can get Brendan to tell me about him."

Ariel's brow shot up. "Which one's Brendan?"

"Come on over, and I'll introduce you."

Ariel grabbed her drink and followed Brie back to the

table where Brendan and Carter waited. "Brendan, Carter, this is my friend, Ariel. Ariel, Brendan and Carter. The rest of the guys had to leave."

"Grab a seat," Brendan said, pointing to an empty chair next to Carter.

"So, what's the deal with Jesse?" Brie asked. She hated asking as she was more interested in Brendan, but she didn't want to lead him on. And she needed to know how to reach Jesse.

Brendan's eyebrow shot up. "Jesse, huh?"

Brie shrugged. "What can I say, I like the strong, silent type."

"He's pretty low key. Goes to work, goes home. Attends church I think. Some Baptist one downtown."

"Oh." This was going to be much harder than Brie had thought. How was she going to just run into him?

"Oh, and he loves coffee. He always goes to this one place, Java Hut, I think it is."

Coffee Brie could do, and it looked like she'd be spending a lot of time at the Java Hut in order to get to know Jesse Calhoun.

3

"Man, you should not have left so early last night," Brendan said as he strapped on his bullet-proof vest. "Brie was interested in you."

"What in the world would I do with a billionaire's daughter?" Jesse strapped on his own vest and closed his locker.

"Um, you could marry her and inherit millions?"

"Unlike you, I hold no desire to marry a woman simply for her money. I want a real woman. One who will go to church with me and be a partner. Not one who's idea of a full day is spending thousands on a new handbag and a pair of shoes."

Brendan slammed his locker shut and fell into step beside Jesse. "You don't even know that she's like that."

• • •

"SHE BOUGHT a round of drinks for a group of men she didn't even know. Not exactly frugal in my book."

Brendan shook his head. "Sometimes, I don't understand you at all, my friend."

"The feeling's mutual." Jesse was cut off from saying anything further as they arrived in the briefing room. The other men were already gathered around the table.

"All right, there's a foreign dignitary in town today, and it's our job to protect him. We will pick him up at the airport, and we will take him to the convention center. Once there, Jesse, you will set up in the lobby. I want you to have eyes on anything that might be able to have eyes on the meeting. Brendan and Carter, you will stay close to the dignitary. The rest of us will be running sweeps on the center. Any questions?"

Jesse glanced at his fellow SWAT members, but as usual, Patrick had made the instructions clear enough that no one had any issues with them.

"Let's mount up."

As Jesse followed the other men out to the SWAT armored vehicle, he prayed silently for their safety. It was a prayer he said every time they rode out in hopes they would all return in the evening.

"So, Brendan, you get a date with the lovely Brie Carter?" Cam asked.

Brendan smiled and shook his head. "Turns out she was more interested in our silent, broody friend here." He jerked his head at Jesse. "But he says he has no use for a billionaire's daughter."

"Ah, you could at least see what she's like, man," Jared said. "Just because she's rich doesn't mean she's not worth knowing. I mean she was definitely easy on the eyes."

"Maybe not, but the ones I've met haven't been very deep. You know I don't care about the latest trends."

"We all know that, Jesse," Carter teased. "It's pretty obvious by the way you dress every day."

"Ha-ha," Jesse shot back. He might not be up on the latest trends, but he wasn't completely inept when it came to fashion.

"Jared's right though man," Patrick said. "I might never have married Tanya if I hadn't given her a chance. She was this sporty jock when I met her, and I thought we would have nothing in common. But her athleticism was just a part of her. It didn't define her."

Jesse supposed they were right. He was making a judgment of Brie without knowing her. "I see your point. If I come across her again, I promise I will at least get to know her."

"That's what I'm talking about." Brendan clapped a hand on his shoulder.

The vehicle rolled to a stop. "Okay, guys. Let's keep eyes open as we enter the airport. We've heard there might be some attacks on this guy's life."

Heads nodded around the vehicle and Jesse touched

the cross that hung around his neck. *Keep us safe, Lord.* Then the door opened, and they filed out.

La Guardia airport was packed as usual, and the team kept a close eye out for any suspect behavior or out of the ordinary events. Patrick led the way to gate 3 and spoke with the agent. The agent nodded and let them into the secure area, so they could meet the dignitary as soon as he disembarked from the plane.

The dignitary was a tall, stern looking Russian, and Jesse could understand why he might need extra guarding with the recent Russian sentiment flooding the country.

"You have him?" The words came from an unassuming muscular man Jesse assumed to be a sky marshal.

"Yes sir, we do." Patrick stepped forward. "Mr. Grigenko if you'll come with us."

The Russian nodded and fell into place behind Patrick. Cam and Carter took up the front flank. Jared and Brendan fell into the back flank and Jesse took his position at the far back. Like a well-oiled machine, the group made their way back through the airport and out to the armored truck.

Jesse was relieved when the door closed, and they were all safe inside. One transport down and only three more to go.

"I REALLY WISH you had picked someone easier," Brie said to Ariel as they sat inside the Java Hut. They'd been there nearly an hour, but no Jesse.

"If I picked someone too easy, it wouldn't be a challenge." Ariel sipped her tall, skinny mocha with no whip. "But I will agree that just sitting here is boring." Her eyes lit up. "I know. Kade is in town filming today. Why don't we go have lunch with him? It might inspire you."

A blush spread across Brie's cheeks, and she ducked her head. Kade Sinclair had been her long-time crush for as long as she could remember. "Do you think he'll have lunch with us?"

Ariel shrugged. "Sure, he will. I'm his little sister, remember." She tapped out a quick text on her phone, and the girls stared at it, waiting for a reply. A moment later it dinged. Ariel scanned the message and smiled. "He has lunch in fifteen minutes and he will meet us at La Porte."

Brie nodded. La Porte was an upscale eatery in the heart of New York City. All the young, trendy people wanted to get in there, but it was generally reserved for the likes of celebrities. Though Brie could probably have gotten in with her last name, Kade was a shoe-in.

The girls finished their coffees and headed out to catch a cab. The bistro wasn't far, but Jimmy Choo shoes were not made for long walks. Thankfully, they had no trouble getting a cab which probably had a lot to do with Ariel's mini skirt and toned legs. Brie had no idea how she wasn't freezing. The air had cooled considerably in the last week, and Brie chose to wear leather pants rather than short skirts. The girls climbed into the cab and exited ten minutes later at the curb of La Porte.

"May I help you?" The hostess asked as they entered. She wore an immaculately pressed white shirt and a bored expression. Her blond hair was pinned up in an elaborate up do.

"Yes, I'm Ariel Sinclair. We're meeting Kade Sinclair for lunch."

The hostess cocked an eyebrow as if she didn't believe her, but she glanced down at her clipboard. "I see a reservation for Kade Sinclair, but he only made a reservation for two."

"Well, we're his guests. He probably just forgot Brie was coming too. This is Brie Carter you know, daughter of Phil Carter."

The hostess looked unimpressed.

"Look, just go ask him. Tell him his sister and Brie are here." Ariel crossed her arms and shot an unpleasant glare in the hostess's direction.

"Give me a moment and I will." The hostess spun and walked away.

"Wow, can you believe the nerve of some people?" Ariel shook her head and ran a hand through her dark locks.

"You didn't tell him I was coming too?" Brie hissed. This was not good. He would think she was just some lame tag-along.

"Relax, I didn't say anything because I assumed he would know you were with me. We're like always together."

Brie shook her head; no longer sure this was a good idea.

A moment later, the hostess reappeared. "I'm sorry for the confusion. If you'll come with me."

She led them towards the back where Kade sat in a far booth. "Ariel, Brie," he said when they sat down.

"Hey, Kade, how is the shoot going today?" Ariel slid in first and Brie scooted next to her.

He shrugged. "Meh, you know. It's work. What are you girls up to today?"

Brie didn't like the way he called them girls as if they were sixteen and still in high school instead of in their mid-twenties.

"Lunch with my favorite brother and then off for some shopping, I suppose." Ariel picked up the menu and scanned it. "Mm, the brioche looks good."

Brie waited for Ariel to steer the conversation to her, so she could contribute something meaningful, but she never did and Kade seemed content to check out the other patrons in the restaurant.

Brie's heart sank as she studied her own menu. What would it take for Kade to notice her?

The waitress appeared a moment later and took their order and still Kade and Ariel seemed content to focus solely on themselves. Ariel raised her phone for a selfie and then jumped on her Snapchat.

Brie would have to speak for herself. "What's the role you're playing now?"

Kade pulled his eyes from something across the restaurant to look at her. "Huh?"

"Your role, what is it?"

"Oh, you know, the usual." He shrugged and returned his attention to something over her shoulder. Brie turned to see what he was looking at and sighed as a group of women came into view. All of them wore low cut shirts and sported much more cleavage than Brie would ever be able to.

Maybe she was just fooling herself. Or maybe she would just have to try harder to get his attention. She tried again. "When is it going to be released?"

His eyes reverted to hers, but just for a moment. "Um, a year, I guess."

Brie rolled her eyes. Talking to him was like trying to pry open a door with a pencil.

After lunch, Ariel hugged Kade goodbye. "Thanks for letting us eat with you, big brother."

"Sure anytime," he said checking his watch. "I gotta run now though."

"Well, that was a total waste," Brie said when he was gone. "He barely even looked at me, and you were no help at all."

Ariel shrugged. "I said I would get you in front of him. The rest is your job."

Brie thought about that on the ride back to her apartment. Maybe a makeover was in order. It seemed Kade was attracted to women with a few more assets than Brie had.

"See you later," Ariel called as Brie climbed out of the cab. Ariel's place was a few blocks up. Brie waved and watched the cab drive away before she entered her building.

When she entered, surprise flooded her to see her father waiting for her in the living room.

"We need to talk, Brie."

A sick sensation erupted in her stomach at the look on his face. He did not seem happy.

"I got the VISA bill in this morning."

Brie's breath caught as she tried to remember what she had purchased recently. There had been that dress and of course a new bag to go with it.

"It was over ten thousand dollars this month, Brie."

Ten thousand? She hadn't thought she had spent that much.

"And I can't keep paying these bills," he continued, "so I think it's time you thought about getting a job."

Brie's eyes bulged, and her mouth dropped open. She leaned back and crossed her slender arms as she regarded her father. "But I don't want to get a job."

He matched her position and narrowed his eyes. "And

I'm tired of funding your every whim. You are twenty-seven years old, Brie. Most people your age have full-time jobs."

Brie pouted her full pink lips. "Well, most people don't have a billionaire father who owns the largest investment company in New York. If they did, they wouldn't have jobs either."

Her father shook his head. He was still distinguished looking, even at nearly fifty. There were white streaks in his dark hair, but Brie thought it made him look more debonair. And he always wore an Armani suit. Those flattered just about everyone, but as her father worked out with a personal trainer, they fit him to a tee.

"I was too easy on you after your mother died. I should have instilled better values in you. Taught you the value of a hard-earned dollar. I didn't get where I've gotten by riding on anyone's coat tail. So, you have two choices. You can get a job, or you can get married, but I'm cutting your money off at the end of the month."

"A month?" Brie flung her arms out to the side. "How am I supposed to find a man who will marry me in a month?" She thought of her bet with Ariel and wondered if she might actually have to go through with marrying Jesse.

"You could start with getting a job," her father said. "I just said one or the other."

"This is so unfair."

"No, what's unfair is you thinking this world revolves

around you. I should have done this a long time ago, but I thought you would see my example and do something with your life. I guess I was wrong. Oh, and by the way, the cut off includes this apartment. So, if you aren't married or don't have a steady job, you'll also need to find a new place to live."

Brie's eyes widened even further. "You would kick your only daughter out on the streets?"

Her father chuckled. "I doubt seriously you would be homeless. You have plenty of wealthy friends who could take you in for a week or two. Right?"

Brie had wealthy friends, but she wasn't sure any of them would let her crash at their place if she didn't have money. Maybe Ariel, but even then, Ariel wouldn't let her stay long. She liked to go out and spend money too much. If Brie didn't have any, she would just be a burden.

"Are you figuring out your friends may only be your friends because of your money?"

"No," Brie protested though that was exactly what she was thinking. "I was just trying to figure out what skills I might have. This is New York, Dad. I can't just waltz in somewhere and get a job."

"Then you start at the bottom like the rest of us did."

The bottom. Of course! Working at a coffee shop certainly felt like the bottom to Brie. But maybe she could make the most of this punishment and kill two birds with one stone. If she could get hired at the coffee place Jesse frequented, she could work on winning him over while satisfying her father. And after all, how hard could it be to make coffee?

"WHAT DO you mean I have no skills?" Brie stared at the young manager who couldn't be much older than she was. "I have an iced, half caff, ristretto, venti, 4-Pump, sugar free, cinnamon, dolce soy skinny latte at least twice a week."

The manager just stared at her. "Just because you order the most obnoxious drink on the menu doesn't mean you know how to make them."

Brie bit her lip. He was right. She had no idea how to make that drink or any other drink, but she needed a job. And she really needed this job for everything to play out right. "Look, I'll make you a deal. One, I promise I will learn how to make these drinks. I may not have many skills, but I can read and comprehend, and I have a good memory. Two, I will post on my social media pages that I will be here every day serving drinks. I promise this place will be flooded with customers."

The manager, whose name was Matt, appeared to consider her offer. "I'll give you one week. You need to know the drinks by then, and I better see an increase in customers."

Brie smiled, and relief flooded her. "I will, and you will. Believe me, this will be good for both of us."

4

"All right guys, nice work with the dignitary today. We're on call for the next few days so enjoy some time at home with your families." Patrick nodded at Cam and Jared. "Or your girlfriends." He pointed to Brendan and Carter. "Or your dog." Patrick caught Jesse's eye and smiled.

"Hey, man, you can't beat the love of a good dog." Jesse knew they were kidding with him. The good-natured ribbing was one thing he loved about being in SWAT. They were so close, they were practically like family. Still, he wished he had someone to go home to.

"Just remember to stay close to your phone in case anything comes up."

Jesse nodded and headed for the locker room to change. His stomach was rumbling, and he really wanted a sandwich and a good cup of coffee.

"So, will you think about giving Brie a chance?" Brendan asked as he fell into step beside Jesse.

"I don't even know how to contact her," Jesse said.

"I got her number if you're interested."

Jesse let out a sigh. Brendan was not going to let this go. "Fine, give me her number. Maybe I'll reach out tomorrow."

"That's all I'm asking. Then if you decide she's not for you, maybe she'll give me a chance."

Jesse stopped and looked at his friend. "You mean you asked her out and she turned you down?"

Brendan shrugged as if this was no big deal. "She said she preferred the strong, silent type. So, please, give her a chance for me?"

Jesse chuckled and shook his head. It wasn't like Brendan didn't have a slew of other women lined up. Of course, they probably weren't billionaires like Brie. And Brendan hated it when women turned him down. "I'll do my best."

"Thanks, my man." Brendan slapped his shoulder and hurried toward the parking lot. He probably had a date waiting already.

Jesse continued into the locker room, showered and changed, and then headed out to his car. He hoped the Java Hut was still open. They made a mean Americano and usually had a sandwich or two left that he could snag for dinner. He didn't mind cooking, but after a long day like today, he just wanted something easy he could eat while watching TV.

"What the?" He did a double take as he passed the building. There was a line out the door. He had never seen it this busy, and while he didn't really want to stand in line for food, he was curious as to the reason for the lengthy wait.

A block over he found a space and parked the car. He pocketed his keys and tugged on his shirt to make sure it covered his concealed weapon. The last thing he needed was someone spotting his weapon and getting stupid in a crowded place like this.

As he joined the back of the line, he tapped the shoulder of the man in front of him. "What's the deal with the crowd? I've never seen it this busy."

The man's eyebrows arched on his forehead. "You mean you didn't hear? Brie Carter is here serving drinks. I'm going to keep this cup forever or maybe sell it on eBay to the highest bidder. Maybe I'll buy two drinks, so I can keep one cup and sell the other."

The man kept rambling, but Jesse stopped listening. What were the odds that Brie would be working here at his favorite coffee shop the night after he met her? Even more ironic was his promise to Brendan to give her a chance. He wasn't sure he would have called her, but now here she was in front of him. Was this a sign? Sign or not, he wanted to see Brie in this environment. He had a feeling she would be frazzled and way out of her league.

His prediction was spot on. As he entered the small room, he could see the frustration on both Brie's face and that of her co-workers. Her blond hair was pulled back in a ponytail, but tendrils stuck out at all sides. Sugar or some similar white substance clung to her cheek.

"No, not like that. You're making an Americano, not a cappuccino." The male employee - Jesse assumed he was the manager - threw up his hands and shook his head.

"I'll get it," Brie said, blowing a puff of air out of her mouth and sending her bangs ruffling.

"It's all right. I don't mind an Americano if Brie is making it." The customer whose drink Brie was working on leaned against the counter and flashed a smile at her.

Jesse rolled his eyes at the man's obvious flirtation. This was just another reason he didn't usually go for girls like Brie. Though he wanted a woman he was physically attracted to, he didn't necessarily want one that everyone was physically attracted to.

It took another ten minutes, but finally Jesse reached the front of the line. "I guess we meet again," he said as Brie turned to him.

"Well, hey, Jesse, nice to see you again. What can I get for you?" She flashed him a tired smile, but Jesse thought it made her look more relatable.

"Americano is my drink, and it seems to be one you've perfected, so I guess I'll stick with that."

"Thank you." Relief was evident in her voice, and he

wondered how many drinks she had messed up since she started.

While she made the drink, he scanned the glass container for a sandwich deciding on a BLT which he handed to her when she returned with his drink. "I'll take this too."

"Are you staying to eat?"

Jesse scanned the room. Though still crowded, the manager had locked the door to new customers and the men were slowly filing out. "Yeah, I could. Why?"

"I'm almost off. I was hoping maybe I could sit with you and relax a little. It's been a long day. I know we don't know each other well, but I don't know anyone else in here, and I'd rather avoid being hit on."

Jesse bit his lip to keep his reply to himself. From the way she dressed and approached their table the night before, he had a hard time believing she didn't enjoy being hit on, but he decided to be nice. "Sure. I'll just be over there. Join me when you can."

A few minutes later, Brie slid into the table across from him and dropped her head onto her hands. Jesse raised an eyebrow and took a sip of his coffee. It wasn't terrible, but it certainly wasn't as good as normal. "Long day?"

"I didn't realize work was so hard," Brie said with a sigh. "I mean I knew work was hard. That's why I avoided it so long, but I didn't know it was this hard."

"So, why did you take the job? You didn't have to, right?"

Brie dropped her eyes to the tabletop. "This is going to sound awful, but my father made me. He said he would take away my money at the end of the month if I didn't get a job by then."

A sarcastic reply bubbled in his throat, but she looked so dejected that he swallowed it and tried for something nicer. "Okay, but why here? Surely pouring coffee isn't your dream job."

Brie's eyes shifted to the side. "I don't have a lot of skills. I pretty much had to beg for this job. In fact, the crowd of people is the only reason I still have a job. I told Matt I would post on social media that I was working here to get people in. At least that worked because I'm fairly certain I do not make good coffee."

"It's not that bad." Jesse offered her a crooked smile. "And if it makes you feel any better, work gets easier the more you do it." He didn't know why, but he felt a little sorry for her.

"I hope so. I'm not sure I can keep doing this all month."

"Don't you have any other skills? Didn't you go to college?"

Brie drug her finger across the table top in an imaginary pattern. "I didn't go to college. It seemed like too much work."

Jesse swallowed a bite of his sandwich. "It's never too late, you know?"

"I know, but I'm not even sure what I want to do. Does that make sense?"

"I'm going to do some community service tomorrow. Why don't you join me? It may not help you decide exactly what you want to do but seeing how those less fortunate live might give you some clarification." Jesse had no idea why the words left his mouth, but it was too late to take them back.

Brie stared into his eyes and took a deep breath. He was sure she was going to say no, that community service was beneath her, but after a moment, she nodded. "Sure, that would be fun."

"Okay. Give me your address, and I'll pick you up tomorrow around ten am."

She held out her hand. "Give me your phone."

"What? Why?"

"So, I can put my number and address in it, of course."

Oh, right, he should have known that. He pulled his phone out of his pocket and handed it across the table to her. With a few quick strokes, she input her details and handed it back to him. "I'm going to go home and shower, but I look forward to seeing you tomorrow."

She pushed back from the table and made her way to the back of the store. Jesse noticed that her walk was different today. Tired and not as cocky. Perhaps there was hope for her yet.

5

Brie woke the next morning achy and sore. She couldn't remember the last time she had stood for so long. A massage was definitely in her future. But not today. Today, she had a date with Jesse, and though community service didn't sound fun, she needed an opportunity to get closer to him to win her bet with Ariel.

She dragged herself out of bed and shuffled to the shower. Hot water would have to do for now. Even though she had showered the previous night when she got home, Brie let the water fall over her for a good ten minutes. It didn't ease all the knots in her muscles, but it helped.

After she finished and dressed, she wandered into the kitchen. Normally, this would be when she either made or ordered herself a cup of coffee, but after working all day yesterday, she had no desire for the brew. Instead, she settled on a chai tea.

She had just finished the warm drink when her intercom sounded.

"Ms. Carter? There is a Jesse Calhoun here to see you." The voice of her doorman echoed throughout the house.

Rinsing the cup quickly, Brie hurried to the front door and pressed the speak button. "Yes, I'm expecting him. Send him up."

She took a moment to check her reflection in the mirror. Her long blond hair had held the curls this morning and they bounced against her shoulders. And the eyeliner she had chosen made her eyes look like emeralds. It was a nice look if she said so herself.

A moment later, the knock came at her door and she opened it to Jesse on the other side.

"Private doorman, huh?" He looked casual in a pair of jeans and a polo shirt.

Brie shrugged and hoped her voice had the nonchalant tone she was going for. "Goes with the territory. Would you like a tour?"

He glanced over her shoulder at the expansive space and shook his head. "I'm good. You ready?"

Brie nodded and followed him into the hall, closing the door behind her, but she couldn't get her mind off his reaction. He hadn't seemed interested in her money at all.

Nor had he wanted to see how big her TV was or how many channels it got. He hadn't asked to sit on her Italian leather couches. It was refreshing, but also… odd. Was he really that unconcerned with whom she was or was he playing her? She'd have to keep a close eye out to discern.

"So, where are we going?" she asked as they stepped into the elevator.

"It's a surprise." He punched the button for the ground floor and said nothing else.

Brie bit her lip. Getting him to open up would be harder than she thought, and she was running out of time.

The doors opened and with a purposeful stride, Jesse crossed the lobby to the front entrance. Brie hurried to keep up with him. As he pushed open the door, the sounds of New York descended upon them. The constant chatter of people on phones, the shuffling of the crowds on the sidewalks, and the sound of car horns stuck in traffic. Brie loved New York, but one reason she loved her penthouse was that it was an escape from the constant noise of New York.

Jesse led the way to a blue truck parked along the street. Not many people in New York drove trucks. They preferred tiny economical cars they could squeeze into tight spots, but somehow the truck fit Jesse. He opened the passenger door for her, and Brie smiled up at him. She was used to having doors opened for her, but mainly because she had a driver. She couldn't remember the last time a date had done so for her unless he also had a driver.

Brie slid into the seat, and Jesse walked around the truck and climbed in the driver's side. He started the engine, and Brie looked over in surprise when Christian music came from the stereo. She supposed she should have expected it since Brendan said he went to church, but Brie knew a lot of people who went to church on Sunday but lived differently during the week.

Even though the traffic was bad, Jesse kept his cool composure as he pulled out into the sea of cars. Nor did he yell angry diatribes when they were stuck for ten minutes in a traffic jam.

"How are you so calm?" she asked when she could contain the curiosity no longer.

Jesse glanced at her out of the corner of his eye before returning his focus to the road. "Well, for one thing my job requires it. I'm the sniper for SWAT, so it's my job to stay somewhere and keep my calm until the action starts. Two, what difference would yelling make? Will it make the cars go any faster?"

"No, I guess not."

"So, why get fired up about it? God is in control, and we'll get there in his time."

"You really believe in God, don't you?"

He glanced at her again. "Do you not?"

Brie took a lock of her blond hair and twirled it in her fingers. "To be honest, I'm not sure. I mean I guess I believe something created this world, but I don't know if I believe in a God who watches out for us."

The corner of Jesse's lip pulled up into a smile. "You've never needed to trust him. Believe me, one day you will, and then you will know he's there."

"Have you? Had that need?"

"Lots of times." He didn't elaborate, and Brie didn't push the subject though she was curious as to what he had faced.

Half an hour later, they pulled up to the children's hospital. A knot of emotion clogged Brie's throat. She had never been in this hospital, but she remembered going to the hospital often when her mother had been sick. And she hadn't stepped foot in one since her mother's death.

"We're going here?" Her voice was pinched and soft.

"Yep, it's what I do when I have time. Bring toys to the kids who are fighting diseases. Some of them have been here so long they start to lose hope. I try to remind them of some simple joys in life.

Brie nodded and tried to swallow her fear. She knew what these kids were going through. Well, not exactly, but close. While she hadn't been the one sick, she had spent enough time watching her mother lose her battle with cancer that she had been one of those kids who gave up hope.

"You okay?"

Brie didn't feel like sharing her sob story with him yet, so she pasted a brave face and a smile on and nodded.

Jesse grabbed several bags from the truck bed and handed them to her to carry. Brie struggled under the weight, but she was determined not to complain as she normally would have done. She could tell Jesse would be turned off if she acted like a spoiled rich girl. He grabbed the remaining bags, twice as many as she had, and led the way to the hospital entrance.

As the hospital doors opened, she struggled to control her breathing. The last thing she needed was to have a panic attack right now.

"Well, hello, Officer Calhoun." A thin black lady smiled and made her way over to Jesse and Brie. "The children will be so happy to see you today."

"Hey, Nancy, sorry it's been so long since I've been in. Work has kept me busy."

"We understand that, and believe me, the kids are happy to see you whenever you make it."

"Thanks." He gestured to Brie. "This is my friend, Brie. She's going to help me deliver toys today."

Nancy turned her kind smile on Brie. "Welcome, Brie. It's about time Officer Calhoun brought a pretty girl with him."

Brie felt her cheeks blush at the insinuation. So, Jesse didn't bring many girls here. That made her feel special, but only for a moment as he jumped in. "Not like that, Nancy. Just friends."

Nancy's face took on one of those 'uh huh sure' expressions, but she nodded and said. "Okay, whatever you say. Let me get you your visitor passes, and you can head on up." She led them over to the desk and tapped on the computer's keyboard. "I know how to spell Officer Calhoun here, but how do you spell your name, hon?"

"B R I E, like the cheese."

Jesse snickered and glanced at her. "Were you named after the cheese?"

Brie put her hands on her hips. "No, it's short for Brienna. It's Celtic and it means strong."

His eyes traveled the length of her body, and he smiled. "You might stick with the cheese story. It's a little more believable."

Brie swatted his arm in mock anger, but she knew he was kidding and as this was the first time she had seen him start to loosen up, she didn't want to break the moment.

"Come on, I want to introduce you to my friends." As Jesse led the way to the elevator, Brie's stomach knotted again. Would she be able to handle seeing kids going through the same pain her mother had?

The doors opened, and they stepped into the elevator. Brie could feel the walls closing in on her. She needed to do something to distract herself. "So, how long have you been doing this?"

"Three years, I guess. My church issued a challenge to do something for someone else, and I wasn't sure what I wanted to do. That night on TV, a commercial came on for St. Jude. I couldn't cure cancer, but I could do something to brighten kids' lives, so I went to a local toy store and bought a ton of toys and brought them in. The toy store found out what I was doing and decided to donate toys after that." He shrugged. "It just kind of took off from there."

Brie cocked her head and studied him. She had never met anyone like Jesse. He willingly gave up his time and money to help others. A tiny piece of her wondered what that would feel like.

When the elevator stopped, they stepped onto the floor. It looked like every other floor except that the walls were more colorful. Painted murals adorned many of them. Jesse stepped up to the desk and addressed the nurse working there.

"Hey, Linda, are there any kids in need of toys today?"

"Jesse!" The woman's eyes lit up and a smile stretched across her lips. "Of course, follow me."

Linda led the way down the hall past several rooms to an open area. Brie was surprised to see a large playroom. It had toys for kids from all ages from a small slide to a video game area. There was even a corner filled with stuffed animals and books. Several children lounged about in the room, but the mood in the room was somber.

"Hey guys, look who's here."

Heads swiveled their direction, and then there was an audible and visible shift. "Officer Calhoun!" The children hurried to him and surrounded him.

"I'll go let some of the others know," Linda said as she touched Jesse's shoulder and then walked away.

"Hey guys, who's ready for some new toys?"

"Me! Me!" It was a resounding chorus as the kids bounced up and down.

Jesse got down on his knees and set down his bags. Surprisingly, the kids didn't tear into them. They waited for him to hand out the goodies. If a child didn't get something they wanted to play with right away, they simply handed it to another child. When his bags were empty, he gestured for Brie to set her bags down.

"This is my friend, Brie, guys. Can you say hi?" The children smiled and waved, and Brie began handing out the toys in her bags as Jesse had. When her hand reached the last toy, she looked up. Only one girl remained in front of her. A little girl of about five with no hair stood in front of her.

"Hi, sweetie, what's your name?"

"Kyla. I have cancer."

Brie's heart broke at the childish innocence. "I'm so sorry, sweetheart. Would you like a doll?" Brie pulled the doll out of the bag and smiled as the girl's eyes lit up.

"Thank you, Ms. Brie." The girl hugged the doll to her chest and walked back to the stuffed animal corner where she sat down and proceeded to play a game with the dolls and animals.

Brie leaned closer to Jesse. "I can see why you do this. They all look so happy, and no one is even fighting."

He flashed her a sad smile. "Yeah, their perspective changes when they are fighting for their lives."

Brie decided at that moment, she was going to do something for these kids. She had the money to spare after all.

They stayed another half hour and then bid their goodbyes to the children. Brie and Jesse were quiet as they left the hospital and walked back to his truck.

"Thank you for bringing me here, but can I ask you a question? How do you keep doing this?"

His eyes caught hers and his brow furrowed slightly. "What do you mean?"

Brie shrugged. "I watched my mom die of cancer and now seeing these kids.... I don't know. It just breaks my heart."

Concern filled Jesse's eyes and he grabbed Brie's hand. "I'm sorry about your mom. I didn't know. I would never have brought you here if I had."

Brie glanced down at their entwined hands. She could feel heat transferring from his hand and slowly climbing up hers. "I'm glad you did. It put things in perspective, but" she paused and dragged her eyes back up to his, "does it ever get easier?"

Jesse took her other hand and pulled her a little closer,

sending a fluttery feeling through her body. What was wrong with her? She wasn't supposed to be feeling anything for him? He was a means to an end.

"I'd love to tell you it does, but I can't. In the three years I've been doing this, I've seen a lot of children recover and go into remission. Those times are amazing because your heart fills with joy for them." His eyes shifted to the side and he cleared his throat before meeting her gaze again, "But I've also seen kids not recover. That's when I'm glad I have my faith to fall back on. It doesn't make the present pain any less, but at least I know they're up in Heaven pain free."

"You really believe that?"

"I do, and so do millions of others. Brie, if there wasn't a loving God watching out for us, then what would be the point of us being here? Our whole lives would simply consist of going through the motions until we died. That may sound nice, doing whatever you want, but it's no life. It has no meaning but believing in Jesus gives meaning to life. During this part, our goal is to strive to be like Him, to show His love to others. But it doesn't end there. We know there's something even better after this life. We get to reign with Jesus forever afterwards in a place with no sin. The way God intended it."

The words were foreign to Brie. Her father had been too busy running his company to ever take her to church, and she didn't remember going with her mother before she died either. But Jesse's face was sincere and there was an honest feeling in his words. "Do you think I could come to church with you one day?" She bit the inside of her lip as she waited for his answer.

His eyes twinkled, and he squeezed her hands, sending another fluttery feeling up her arms. "I'd love to take you to church with me. How about this Sunday?"

Brie nodded and stared up at him. They were in a moment and she knew he could feel it too. She parted her lips, willing him to kiss her. She wanted to know if his mouth would elicit a fire into her the way his hands did, but after a moment of his eyes staring into hers, he dropped her hands and opened the truck door for her.

Brie blinked. Had she imagined it then? His attraction? And why wasn't he falling for her the way other men did? Brie had never had an issue getting a man to kiss her. Until now. Now, she had been turned down by both Kade and Jesse in less than two days. Confused, she climbed up into the truck and folded her hands into her lap. Maybe he was only looking for friendship.

The ride back to her apartment was quiet which made Brie feel worse. She had nothing to do but rehash the feelings and replay the moments over in her head and wonder what went wrong.

When he finally found a parking spot on her street, she reached for her handle, but Jesse stayed her arm. "Wait, Brie, let me walk you up."

She shook her head, tears pricking her eyes. "No, that's not necessary."

"It is because I need to tell you something. Please."

Brie shrugged and blinked to keep the tears back. "Fine, if you want."

She stepped out of the truck and waited for him to catch up to her. Then they walked back to her apartment in silence. When they reached her door, she turned to him. "So, what did you need to tell me?"

He stepped toward her and reached his hand around, cupping her neck and tilting her face up. Brie's breath caught in her throat. "I wanted to tell you that I don't kiss lightly. When I kiss someone, it means something, and when I first met you, I couldn't imagine kissing you. But I saw someone different today. Someone I could date, but I want to be sure, do you understand?"

The fingers of his other hand traced her lips, sending chills down Brie's spine. An intensity blazed in his eyes that threw her heart into overdrive. She had never felt so connected to someone whom she hadn't kissed. All she could do was nod. Her ability to speak was lost in the feelings between them.

"Good. Now, I'd like to see you again, so how about tomorrow if I don't get called in?"

"I'd like that," Brie managed to whisper.

Jesse brushed her lips with his finger one last time before he released her and stepped back. "Then I'll call you later." Before she could say anything else, he turned and walked to the elevator. His shoulders and neck were stiff as if he was fighting his own emotion.

Brie leaned against her apartment door and put her hand over her chest. Her heart thudded against it. She had never felt anything like that, and now she was certain that kissing Jesse might not only be explosive but addictive as well.

6

Jesse woke the next morning with Brie on his mind. He hadn't thought there was anything to her, much less anything that would interest him. But she had been different. Maybe it was having to get a job. Maybe it was meeting the kids. Whatever it was, he had enjoyed spending the day with her yesterday, and he couldn't wait to see her again today.

Maybe he could take her to the park. He rarely got a chance to take Bugsy to the park and let him spend some energy. And if he was honestly thinking about a relationship with Brie, he needed to know she liked dogs. Or at least his dog.

He rolled over and scratched the Boston Terrier behind the ears. Jesse hadn't planned on letting a dog share his bed, but Bugsy had never taken to the dog bed Jesse had bought for him. After a few nights of continually putting the dog on the floor and listening to him whine, Jesse had broken down and allowed the dog to sleep on the bed.

Jesse twisted back to glance at the clock on his nightstand, but it didn't read nine am yet. He refused to call Brie before nine in case she slept in, but surely a text wouldn't wake her. Unplugging his phone from the charger, he tapped a quick message to her.

Would you care to accompany Bugsy and I to the park today?

He wasn't expecting a response, but his phone buzzed a moment later.

I'd love to, but I work until four. Can we do dinner instead?

Dinner would work if he could convince her to come to his place. Would she be up for that? Or would she be expecting him to take her to some fancy restaurant? Could he even afford to take her to some fancy restaurant?

Can I cook for you here?

Sure, gotta run.

"Hm, well, all right. I guess maybe she can do down-to-earth things too, Bugsy. Let me get cleaned up and then we'll run some errands and let you play."

Bugsy looked up briefly before laying his head back down and closing his eyes. Jesse shook his head as he pushed back the blue comforter and sheets and got out of bed. The dog was barely five but acted like an old man sometimes.

After a shower and a quick breakfast, he loaded Bugsy

up in his truck and headed to the store. He rarely had time to run errands during the week and his empty cupboards showed it. His dry cereal would have tasted much better with milk this morning. Not to mention his coffee.

Jesse had opted to live in one of the suburbs of New Jersey instead of New York itself. He liked being close to the city for the entertainment, but he hated the traffic having grown up in rural Montana. Besides, one day he hoped to have a wife and children, and he did not want them growing up in some high-rise apartment without a yard to play in.

He parked in the store lot, glad that the cool air would not only keep Bugsy safe while he was inside but also keep his groceries cold while they played at the park. Jesse loved winter, at least until the snow hindered his job. Then it became an obnoxious dirty mess.

The doors to the store whooshed open and Jesse grabbed a small cart. He had no idea what to fix Brie, but he assumed she ate healthy. Either that or she had an amazing metabolism to stay so thin. So, anything loaded with carbs was probably out. Thankfully, Jesse had once been an amateur boxer, and he knew how to eat healthy. He headed for the vegetable aisle and stocked up on lettuce, tomatoes, onions, and spices. Then he grabbed a package of chicken breasts and a loaf of French bread just in case. With the dinner items in his basket, he grabbed the few other groceries he needed. There was no telling when he'd get another day like this to stock up.

After paying for the groceries, he headed back to his car. Bugsy stood faithfully at the passenger window, his face pressed against the glass. When he saw Jesse, his active tongue licked the window. Jesse shook his head as he loaded the groceries in the bed of the truck. He'd have to wash the windows again, but that was a pretty common occurrence where Bugsy was concerned.

With the bags secured, Jesse climbed back in the truck and headed to the closest park. He pulled into a spot and parked before clicking on Bugsy's leash and letting the dog out of the truck. Bugsy wasn't the type to take off like a rocket, but New York had strict leash laws and the last thing Jesse needed was a citation on his record.

The park was rather empty today. A few die-hard runners jogged the nearby track, and some of the park benches were filled with people either reading or glued to their cell phones. Jesse walked Bugsy to the leash free enclosure in the park and removed the leash. Then he grabbed the ball he had shoved in his pocket from the truck and tossed it for the dog. Bugsy was terrible at fetching, but he loved to go after the ball and chew on it.

"Ah, your dog is so cute."

Jesse turned to see a perky brunette at his side. She held a small white teacup Pomeranian in her arms and a flirtatious expression on her face. He was used to this reaction from women, but never really understood it.

What was it about a dog that made a man more attractive to them?

"Uh, thanks. Yours is too." Jesse did not understand teacup dogs. They required nearly constant supervision and didn't live half as long as other dogs. However, they appeared to be trendy with the elite of New York.

The girl smiled and nuzzled her tiny dog. "This is Trixie, and I'm Kimber." She put out her hand, a slender one with perfectly manicured nails.

"Nice to meet you. I'm Jesse." He shook her hand, careful not to squeeze too tightly. She looked fragile, and he didn't want to break her.

"Wow, you have such strong hands." She batted her overdone lashes at him, and Jesse tried to suppress his sigh. Why did all the women he met in New York seem like dressed up Barbie dolls to him? Why couldn't he meet someone down to earth? Like the girls from Montana.

"Yes, well, nice to meet you. I better go rescue his ball before he destroys it." Jesse flashed a wave and a smile, so as not to appear too rude and then jogged over to where Bugsy was chewing on his ball. "Here boy, let's try again." He tugged the ball from the dog's mouth and threw it farther away to add even more distance between the brunette and himself.

After half an hour of chasing the ball, Bugsy lay down on the ground. "All right, boy, you ready to go back home?" The dog looked up at him and slowly stood back up. Jesse leaned down and lifted Bugsy into his arms. "It's my fault, boy. I don't get to exercise you the way I would like. Maybe I'll see if I can get you a dog walker."

Jesse carried the dog back to the truck. Before they got home, Bugsy had curled up and fallen asleep on the passenger seat. He let him continue sleeping while he carried the groceries inside and then came back for the dog. Bugsy looked up briefly as he laid him on the couch but quickly closed his eyes again.

Jesse returned to the kitchen to put the groceries away and prep for dinner.

BRIE TOOK off her shoes and put her feet in her soaking bath. She'd messed up slightly fewer coffees today, but she still had spent most of the day on her feet, and they were complaining. She wasn't sure she would be able to do this coffee thing much longer. Unfortunately, her father's ultimatum echoed in her head. She either had to have a job or a husband at the end of the month.

Her cell phone rang in her pocket, and she fished it out. "Hello?"

"Brie, what are you doing? There is going to be an epic party tonight at this old abandoned warehouse." Ariel's voice was chipper and spunky on the other end of the phone. She probably hadn't done any work today. Brie envied her friend and wondered if she'd ever get back to those carefree days.

"I can't Ariel. I just got off work, and I'm meeting Jesse tonight."

"Work? What are you talking about?"

Brie sighed. "I spent too much money last month, and Dad threatened to cut off my supply if I didn't get a job or get married. Since I had no one to marry right away, I had to get a job."

"Ugh, that blows. What are you doing?"

"I'm working at the Java Hut. Didn't you see my posts the other day?" She knew she had been busy, but how had her best friend missed all her social media posts about the job?

"Briefly, but I thought you were just doing some charity thing. I didn't really pay attention."

Ariel's words rubbed like sandpaper. Her best friend hadn't paid attention? "Well, it wasn't, and since I needed a job, I figured I might as well find one that would allow me to interact with Jesse as well."

"Fine. Fine. Go on your date. I'll tell you all about it tomorrow."

Brie sighed and rolled her eyes. "I have to work tomorrow, but we'll catch up soon."

She hung up the phone and wiggled her toes in the warm water for a moment longer before deciding she needed to get up and take a shower.

An hour later she stood in front of Jesse's door. He had texted over his address, and Brie had taken a cab to his house. She would have taken one of her father's limos, but after the credit card fiasco, she feared spending too much of his money. Thankfully, she'd had enough cash lying around to pay for the cab, but she would probably have to ask Jesse for a ride back.

She took a deep breath and rang the bell. From inside the house she heard barking and gripped her purse tighter. She wasn't a big fan of dogs.

The door swung open and Jesse stood on the other side. At his feet was a Boston Terrier. Brie relaxed. At least it was a small dog. She liked those a little better.

"Hey, I hope you're hungry." He stepped back allowing her entrance.

Brie's stomach rumbled, and she smiled. "I guess I am. I'm pretty sure I worked through lunch."

"Yep, I do that a lot myself. I'd say you get used to it, but you never really do."

As he led the way to his kitchen, Brie took in the surroundings. It wasn't a big place, nothing like her apartment, but it had a homey feel. Though definitely much more masculine. Where she would have had pinks and creams, he had blues and browns. A large pair of deer antlers hung over his fireplace and above that a shelf lined with medals and trophies. She wondered what they were for.

"I wasn't sure what you eat, you know if you're on a special diet or anything-"

Brie's eyebrows arched. "You think I need to diet?"

A soft pink color spread across Jesse's cheeks, highlighting the row of freckles across his nose. "No, I think you look great, er fine, uh never mind."

Brie bit back her smile. She enjoyed being able to fluster him, but she didn't want him to know that.

"Anyway, I have bruschetta chicken, salad, and bread."

Brie didn't eat bread. One of the ways she stayed so slim was watching her carbs, but she wasn't about to tell him that now. She just wouldn't put any on her plate. "Sounds wonderful."

He held out a chair for her and scooted her in after she sat. Brie liked this gesture. She couldn't remember the last time a man had done it for her, and it made her feel special. Kade would probably never do that. She began to wonder why she was fascinated with Kade after all.

Jesse turned to the stove and returned a moment later with a plate. A chicken breast smothered in tomatoes and basil lay in the middle of the plate. "There's cheese on the table if you want to add some on. It should be hot enough to melt still." He put a bowl of salad in the middle, another bowl with cut up French bread next to it, and then sat down across from her with his own plate.

"This smells delicious. Where did you learn to cook?"

"My mom. I grew up with a big family, and since I was the second oldest child, she taught my brother and I both to cook at a young age, so we could help out. Shall we pray so we can eat?"

"Uh, sure." Brie still wasn't sure about this prayer thing, but she needed Jesse to believe she was.

"Heavenly Father, we thank you for this food, for the good company, and for the many blessings you've given us. Amen."

"Amen," Brie echoed hoping that was the right thing to do. She cut into her chicken and took a bite. The flavors danced in her mouth. Balsamic vinaigrette paired with basil, garlic, and tomatoes. It tasted similar to pricey dishes she'd eaten in Italy during their trip there one year.

"So, does your family live here?" she asked when she finished chewing the bite.

He shook his head and finished his own bite. "No, most of them still live in Montana where I'm from. I wanted to see what the world had to offer, so I moved to the biggest city I could think of." He smiled. "Ended up here in New York. Joined SWAT and haven't left since."

"You don't have any family around here?" Brie couldn't imagine not having the support of her father. He worked long hours, but he always made sure he was off for holidays, so they could spend them together. At least he had after her mother died.

"I have my SWAT family, and I try to get home when I have the time. It's hard though as we are often on call." As if on cue, his cell phone rang, and Jesse's demeanor shifted from relaxed to super focused. He answered his phone, his voice low and serious. "Calhoun here.... Right....be right there boss." He shoved the phone back in his pocket and pushed his chair back. "Sorry, Brie, we'll have to take a raincheck. Duty calls."

"Oh, okay, do you think I can ride in with you though? I took a cab here and wherever your headquarters are will probably be closer to my apartment." She hated asking especially since he looked like time was important, but she didn't have the money for a return trip and she didn't want to ask her father.

"I'll take you to the station and see if one of the guy's wives can take you home from there."

"Sure, that will be fine. Thank you for the dinner." She looked longingly at the chicken she didn't get to finish as she pushed back from the table.

After strapping on his weapon and grabbing a duffel bag from behind his couch, he opened the door and waited for her to exit before locking it. She wondered what was in the bag but decided she probably didn't want to know. Guns made her nervous, and her heart was already speeding up from the one on his hip.

He tossed the bag in the truck bed and opened her door. "Here, text Cam and ask if Cara can meet us at the station." He handed her his phone as she climbed in.

Brie stared at the phone. What was she supposed to say? She didn't know Cam other than the few minutes she had spent with him at the bar, and she hadn't been focused on him. She wasn't even entirely sure which one he was.

Jesse swung open the driver's side door, climbed inside, and fired the engine up. A moment later, they were pulling out of his driveway and roaring down the street.

Brie tapped the screen and found her way to his contacts, then scrolled down until she found Cam's number. She paused, trying to think of what to say.

Can Cara meet us at the station? I need a favor.

It was simple and to the point. With the message sent, she handed the phone back to Jesse who took it and shoved it back in his pocket. His eyes never left the road.

Twenty minutes later, they pulled into the station lot and Jesse parked the truck. After opening her door, he grabbed his bag from the bed and led the way inside. Brie followed, unsure what she was supposed to be doing.

Jesse pulled the door open to a small lobby decorated mainly in grey. A few chairs sat in the lobby as well as a desk that served as a check in. A woman with frizzy red hair and sixty style glasses sat behind the desk, a pencil sticking out of her hair.

"Hey Penny," Jesse said as he approached her. "This is my friend Brie. She had to come with me, but Cara is coming to pick her up. Can you keep her company until then?"

"Oh, of course. I love meeting new people. Hi, my name is Penelope, but everyone calls me Penny." The woman stood and stretched out a hand. Every nail was painted a different color which matched her colorful outfit. She must be quite the personality.

"I'm so sorry, Brie, but I have to go." He threw a wave her direction and disappeared through a door.

"So, tell me about yourself, Brie," Penny said as the women shook hands.

7

Cam met Jesse as soon as he stepped through the door. "I got your message and Cara will be here shortly. She had to get some gas on the way."

"No worries, and thanks man. I've got Penny keeping Brie company."

Cam's brow arched, and he rubbed his strong chin. "Brie, huh? Decide to give the girl a chance after all?"

Jesse shrugged. "I saw a different side of her. I'm still not sure, but I'm taking the opportunity to get to know her."

"Right on, man. Sometimes they surprise you." Cam clapped him on the shoulder and the two joined the rest of the men in the briefing room.

"Good, everyone's here," Patrick said when they entered. "We've got a situation at the penitentiary. Some inmates escaped their cells and have the place on lockdown. I'm not going to lie. This will be dangerous and a long night."

"We're ready, boss," Brendan said.

The rest of the group nodded, and they all headed to the weapon room to mount up.

"AH, HERE SHE IS," Penny said as a petite blond opened the front door. "Cara, this is Brie."

Cara was nothing like Brie imagined. Cam was so large and muscular, and Cara was tiny. He must dwarf her.

"Nice to meet you, Brie. I hear you need a ride." Cara stuck out her hand and Brie shook it. She had a slight southern accent, and Brie wondered how she and Cam had met.

"If you don't mind. I told Jesse I could take a cab from here, but he insisted I ask one of you."

Cara smiled and winked at Penny. "Yep, that's our Jesse. Always the gentleman. I have to say, it's nice to finally see him with a girl. We've wanted him to find a nice one for so long."

Brie swallowed the knot in her throat. Suddenly she felt awful; she wasn't being nice. She had started seeing him on a bet, but now she was no longer sure she wanted to go through with it. Jesse was a nice guy, and his friends were going out of their way to help her even though they didn't know her. She would have to tell Ariel the bet was off.

"So, he doesn't bring girls here very often?" Brie would feel even worse if he didn't date much.

Cara chuckled. "Honey, he's never brought a girl here. In fact, I've only heard Cam mention a girl once or twice."

Brie felt like scum. She wasn't sure how she felt about Jesse romantically, but she enjoyed his company. Not only would she have to call off the bet, but she'd have to make sure he never found out about it.

"Anyway, you ready?"

Brie nodded and followed Cara out to her car. "Where to?" she asked as the girls buckled in.

"71 Laight Street."

Cara performed a double take and let out a low whistle. "Whoa, that's upscale. I gotta say. I did not expect that. Jesse is usually much more low key."

Brie blushed. "It's my father's money. I certainly haven't earned any of it." She had never thought about the image she emitted because all her friends were the same but seeing herself through Jesse's and his friends' eyes made her feel like the snobby rich girl he had thought she was. In truth, she was that girl, but she was beginning to desire something more. Something that made her Brie Carter instead of billionaire Phil Carter's daughter. If only she knew what that was.

THE SWAT SUV rolled up to the penitentiary and Patrick began calling out instructions. "Jared, you and Carter are with me. We'll take cell block A. Cam, Brendan, and Jesse, you take cell block B." He handed a tablet to Cam, who shoved it in an interior pocket of his jacket. "Inmate and guard photos are uploaded. You check everyone. Don't just accept a guard at face value. We're looking for four inmates in particular." He read their names and flashed their pictures up for the men to see. "Communication will be via radio, so make sure you have your ears in. Keep your eyes open and watch each other's backs."

The group nodded and separated into their teams. Jesse sent up a silent prayer for everyone's safety as he followed Cam and Brendan into the building. An eerie feeling descended as they walked inside. Silence abounded, and a red light flashed as the only warning that something was wrong. Cam took the lead with his rifle in front. Brendan took the middle position, and Jesse brought up the rear. It was a position that took time to get used to as he needed to walk backwards most of the time to keep their flank protected.

The hallway opened into a large room and a commotion off to the right grabbed their attention.

"This is the New York SWAT team," Cam called. "Come out with your hands up."

"We're not going back in," a voice called back. "Ya'll

gonna have to kill us first."

"No one wants to kill anybody today," Cam hollered back. "You guys just put down any weapons that you have and come out nice and easy."

The response was a round of gunfire in their direction. Jesse, Brendan, and Cam rolled into position and fired back, trying to aim low to injure and not kill.

When the shots ceased, Jesse heard a different voice. "Come on, man, they've got more firepower than we do. I don't want to die today."

"Fine." The voice was low and angry, but a gun clattered to the floor and soon slid into view from the inmate's kick.

Brendan took the lead in retrieving the weapon as Cam and Jesse covered his back. A minute later, two inmates came out from behind the half wall. One was bleeding from his shoulder. The other from a shot to the leg.

"Get them patched up, Jesse. I'll send over what we have to Pat."

Jesse pulled the medical bag out of his pack and assessed the two men. The leg injury appeared worse, so while Brendan held a gun on both inmates, Jesse retrieved the gauze and began attending to the wound.

"Why are you fixing us up?" the man asked. "We were set to kill you."

Jesse looked up at the man who had gang tattoos on his face and lower arms. He had probably lived a hard life. "Because my partner was right. We don't want to take lives. Sometimes we must to defend ourselves, but our job is to save as many as we can. As a unit and a decent human being, we couldn't stand here and watch you bleed to death. Whatever you've done to land here, you're still a human being who deserves the same rights to care as everyone else."

The inmate looked at him with narrowed eyes. "I've never met anyone who speaks like you. What makes you so different?"

Jesse finished wrapping the wound as he contemplated how much he should say. He chose to keep it simple. "God."

"WHAT DO you mean you want to call the bet off?" Ariel asked as they sat in Brie's heat-controlled pool. The outside air might be cool, but she was able to control the temperature of her deck and that of the pool. "It's only been like four days."

"I know," she stretched out her aching shoulders, "but he's really nice. Cam's wife drove me home from the station today when Jesse got called in, and she didn't even know me. How many people do we know who would do that?"

Ariel shrugged. "I would send my driver for the right price."

"That's just it," Brie said with a shake of her head, "she didn't take any money. She did it for free."

"How can you expect to get ahead that way?"

"I don't think they expect to get ahead. They seem happy where they are. Also, Cara told me Jesse never brought girls there. It just seems too mean."

"But what about Kade?"

Brie shrugged. "I don't know. If it's meant to be, it will work out, but I'm kinda enjoying getting to know Jesse."

Ariel's brows knitted together. "You can't be serious. Brie, it was supposed to just be a bet. Have you even kissed this guy yet?"

"Not yet. He said he doesn't kiss unless he's sure he could see a relationship."

Ariel's nose wrinkled in an unattractive gesture. "Why would he do that? If I don't like the way a guy kisses, then I know there's no need to pursue a relationship. I would hate to invest all that work and then find out he kissed like a slobbery dog or something."

Brie arched an eyebrow at Ariel. She couldn't remember the last time Ariel had invested in a relationship unless it was with her poodle. And while she could see her point, Brie thought it was kind of sweet that Jesse waited. At least that way he wasn't kissing half of New York like some people she knew.

"You're going to keep seeing him, aren't you?"

Brie shrugged. She wanted to see Jesse again, but she didn't like having to defend herself to Ariel.

8

Jesse felt stiff and sweaty as they rode back to the station early the next morning. The mishap at the penitentiary had taken almost ten hours to get completely under control. Thankfully, no one had been seriously injured and all the inmates were accounted for and back in their cells.

"That was good work in there everyone," Patrick said looking at each man in turn. "I know tomorrow is Sunday, but we are on call again, so get some rest when you get home and make sure your phones are with you."

"You gonna see Brie again?" Cam asked leaning closer to Jesse.

"Probably not today. I'm too tired, but I invited her to church with me tomorrow."

Cam whistled softly. "Church already? You're gonna scare the poor girl away."

Jesse shook his head. "Nah, any girl who won't go to church with me isn't someone I want to date anyway."

Cam chuckled. "Yeah, okay, if you say so, man."

"Hey, thanks again for Cara picking her up. Not the way I wanted our date to end, but such is the way it goes."

"No worries, man, I got your back and believe me, Cara knows only too well how that happens. She probably explained it all to Brie if she didn't scare her away. Being married to a SWAT member takes a special kind of woman."

Jesse knew that was true. It was one reason he was so careful. His own mother had been married three times, and while he enjoyed having lots of siblings, the divorces had rocked the house each time. He planned to make his marriage last if he was lucky enough to find a wife, but Cam was right. It wasn't easy being married to a SWAT member. They could rarely plan vacations because they were almost always on call, and he couldn't count how many birthdays and anniversaries the other guys had missed. A woman had to be independent and understanding, and Jesse wasn't sure Brie was. But, something about her intrigued him. So, he would give it a few more days and a lot more prayer.

When they returned to the station, Jesse forced himself to shower before heading home. Not only did he need to wash off the grime, but the hot water would wake him up enough for the drive home.

"She seems lovely," Penny said as he passed the reception desk on the way back out.

"Yeah?" Jesse didn't need Penny's approval, but he knew she believed like he did, so it carried more weight than some of the guys.

"I mean I didn't see her in her natural element, but yeah. She appeared smart and nice. Does she go to church?"

"She's coming with me tomorrow."

Penny flashed a thumb up sign, and Jesse shook his head as he walked off. He didn't know many other thirty-year-old women who flashed thumb up signs anymore, but Penny walked to her own drum. It was one of her more endearing qualities.

Bugsy greeted him when he arrived home, and after a quick sandwich to tide the growling monster in his stomach - he never had finished dinner - he brushed his teeth and crawled in bed. He didn't think he would sleep the whole day, but just in case he set his alarm for the following morning and sent Brie a quick text letting her know he would pick her up at nine thirty on his way to church if she still wanted to come.

BRIE SMILED at the text on her phone again. Though still a little nervous about going to church, she looked forward to seeing Jesse again, especially after their last time together got cut short.

"Aren't you going to buy anything?" Ariel asked as she held up a designer dress.

"I'd love to, but I can't." Brie's father hadn't explicitly said she couldn't buy anything else, but she was pretty sure that his ultimatum included that detail. Besides, she didn't need anything else. Brie realized some of her shopping had been out of boredom, but since having to get a job, she didn't find herself bored very often. Tired? Yes, but bored? Not so much.

"Come on. Just a little something small for yourself?" Ariel scanned the shelves and grabbed a small bag. "Here, how about this?"

Brie shook her head. "I don't need a new bag. Besides," she leaned in and turned the price tag over, "it's two thousand dollars. My dad made me get a job because I spent too much, remember?"

Ariel rolled her eyes. "You're no fun anymore. Fine, I'll get it for both of us. It will look great with my outfit for the party tonight. You are still coming, aren't you?"

Brie hesitated. She did want to go out after a long week of work, but she didn't want to be out too late since she was attending church with Jesse. The last thing she needed was to show up with dark circles under her eyes.

"You can't skip the party. It's like the biggest event since… since…"

"Since the last event?" Brie supplied with a smile. The

party was going to be big, but not the event Ariel was making it out to be.

"Kade will be there." A mischievous smile crossed Ariel's face.

Conflicting emotions battled inside Brie. She did want to see Kade again, didn't she? "I'm coming. I just can't stay all night because I'm seeing Jesse in the morning."

"On Sunday? Where could you possibly be going on Sunday morning?" Her eyes widened as the only logical conclusion came to mind. "You're going to church with him?"

Brie shrugged.

"Why? You called the bet off. It's not like you have to keep trying to impress him."

"I'd already agreed to go. It would be rude not to."

Ariel shook her head. "Who are you? And what did you do with my friend?"

Brie knew Ariel was teasing, but she was beginning to wonder the same thing. Ever since she had gone to the children's hospital with Jesse, she couldn't get those kids out of her head. She wanted to do something for them. Something like Jesse did. She'd have to discuss ideas with her father. He didn't want her spending money frivolously, but surely, he wouldn't be against a donation to the hospital.

"I'm still here." Brie glanced at her watch. She still needed to shower after her shift this morning. She had met Ariel right after she got off. "Shouldn't we get ready for that party now?"

"Fine, let me check out, and then we can swing by your place. I'm assuming you want to get cleaned up first."

Brie did not miss the disdain in her friend's voice, and it irritated her. Just because Ariel didn't have to work didn't mean she needed to make fun of Brie for it. It wasn't like it had been her idea although she did get some satisfaction out of it. Even though being a barista wasn't her dream, she had felt good the first time she got someone's drink order right and the first day she made every drink right.

"Of course. I hadn't planned on going without a shower."

"Good, because no offense, but you smell like sweat and vanilla syrup." Arms laden, Ariel made her way to the register and Brie shook her head as she followed. Why did people say no offense when they clearly meant it to be offensive? Had she been like that?

A few minutes later, shopping bags in hand, Ariel led the way to her father's limo and the girls climbed inside.

After a quick stop at Brie's for her to shower and change, the girls were back on the road and headed to the upper east side for the party. The driver pulled up to the club and the girls got out. Music carried out onto the streets and the line to get in wrapped around the building.

Brie checked her watch again. It was almost ten and she wanted to be home by midnight at the very latest. But with this line, they might not even make it inside by midnight. "Ariel, are you sure you want to go to this? We might not even get in."

"Oh, we'll get in. Watch me." Ariel strode purposefully to the front of the line, her long legs pumping underneath her mini skirt.

"Hey, there's a line," a guy called from the line as Ariel reached the front.

"Not for me." She smiled sweetly at the man and then turned to the very muscular bouncer. "I'm Ariel Sinclair. Kade Sinclair's sister. He should have my friend Brie and me as his guests."

The bouncer scanned the list, and after looking at their IDs, he let them in.

"Did you tell Kade I was coming with you?" Brie asked as they entered.

"No, but he knows we're always together. You do still want Kade, don't you?"

"I..." Brie had no answer for that. Did she still want him or did she just like the idea of him? Kade had never paid attention to her, but Jesse opened doors for her and cooked for her. However, Jesse didn't have the money she was used to, nor did he have any connections. Maybe it wouldn't hurt to give Kade one more shot.

They found him upstairs in a corner booth surrounded by women. Brie sighed as she looked over the competition. All of them wore skin tight clothing and had many more assets than Brie did. She glanced down at her own dress. It was a designer dress, but Brie had never gone for the ultra-skin-tight clothing.

"Hey Kade, thanks for the add," Ariel said.

"Sure." He waved his hand in a dismissive gesture before placing it around the shoulders of one of the women and pulling her in for a kiss.

Brie's stomach turned, and she wondered what she had been thinking wanting to date him. She didn't want to just be a trophy on someone's arm, and that's exactly what these women looked like. "Let's go dance," she said to Ariel.

Ariel nodded, and the girls headed back downstairs. The dance floor was crowded, and they had a hard time finding a place to call their own. When they finally did, Brie tried to relax, but the club was so loud, and the flashing lights bothered her eyes. What was wrong with her? She used to love going dancing, hadn't she? But as she thought back, she realized dancing had always been Ariel's idea. Brie had gone along because she felt like she needed to. That's what you did when you were rich. You made appearances at the hippest clubs, so you could be seen.

But suddenly she didn't feel the need to be seen. "Hey, I'm going to head home," Brie hollered to Ariel. The music was so loud that she couldn't barely hear her own thoughts.

"What?"

"I'm heading home. I'll talk to you later."

"We just got here."

Brie shrugged. "I'm just not feeling it tonight."

"Your loss," Ariel said as a handsome man tapped her on the shoulder. With a smile, she turned her attention to him, and Brie was no longer a thought on her mind.

Brie shook her head and walked toward the exit. Maybe it was being forced to get a job, or meeting Jesse and the kids, but she was beginning to wonder what she was doing. She pulled her phone out of her purse and called her father's limo service. Brie wasn't sure she would be able to find a cab, and there was no way she was walking the streets in an unfamiliar area at night.

9

Jesse pulled up in front of Brie's building the next morning excited and a little nervous. Today would be a defining day though Brie had no idea. If she liked his church and saw herself continuing to come with him, he was prepared to start dating her, but if she couldn't, he would end it now before his feelings grew anymore.

He parked the truck, whispered a quick prayer, and headed inside. "Can you ring Brie Carter and tell her Jesse Calhoun is here?" he asked the man behind the front desk this morning. He still found it odd he couldn't just go up to her apartment, but he supposed with her money and family name, she needed to be extra careful.

The man nodded and picked up a phone. "Ms. Carter, there is a Jesse Calhoun here for you. Yes, ma'am." He placed the phone down and regarded Jesse again. "You may go up. I assume you know the floor."

"Yes, thank you." Jesse flashed a smile and headed for the elevator. A moment later, he stood in front of Brie's door. He took a moment to scan his shirt and pants for any loose dog hair before ringing the bell. Bugsy didn't shed much, but occasionally, he would find stray hairs on his clothing, and he wanted to make sure he had none today.

The door swung open and Brie smiled at him from the other side. Her blond hair was curled and hung loose around her shoulders, and she wore a pale pink dress that brought out the sparkle in her eyes.

"You look beautiful," he said.

A soft pink color flooded her face, and she looked away. "Are you sure? I wasn't sure what to wear to church. It's been so long since I was in one."

"Well, God doesn't care what you wear to church, but yes, you look amazing." Though his church was laid back and many women wore pants and even jeans, Jesse always admired the women who dressed more femininely and wore skirts and dresses. Maybe it was old fashioned, but he appreciated the differences between men and women. "You might want to grab a coat though. It was snowing on the way over here, and I'm not sure how much we're supposed to get."

"Right, thank you." Brie ducked inside and moments later returned with an expensive looking designer coat.

Though Jesse would never be able to afford one like it, he had to admit it hugged her in all the right places.

As they walked back to the elevator, he couldn't help wondering if her money and his lack of it would come between them. He made decent money on SWAT, but nowhere near what she was used to. If they did date, would she expect elaborate outings and expensive jewelry? And what if she invited him into her world? Would he fit in with her rich friends? He pushed the insecurities aside as he pushed the elevator button. They could wait. First, he had to see how church went.

The falling snow made the drive a little slower, but half an hour later, they arrived. Jesse attended a smaller Nazarene church on the outskirts of the city. He liked that it wasn't in the city traffic, and he didn't have to worry about parking.

The building sat on about an acre, a large rectangular building with three crosses on top, but it had a playground for the kids, a small field, and a parking lot. More than any church in the city had.

Jesse parked the truck and hurried to Brie's side to open the door. He wished he had brought an umbrella as the snow was coming down harder now. "Want to make a run for it?"

Brie shook her head, a small smile pulling at the corners of her mouth. "I love the snow. Let's just enjoy it."

Jesse tilted his head at her. He had not expected that at

all. Had he been wrong about Brie originally or was she changing in front of his eyes? "All right, come on." He held out his hand, and she placed hers in his palm. Warmth traveled up his arm and he shifted his hand, so their fingers were intertwined. She winked at him, and hand-in-hand, they walked into the church.

Greeters stood under the awning holding umbrellas, and one hurried their way as he noticed them, but Jesse waved him off. "We're enjoying the snow but thank you." Beside him, Brie giggled and tilted her face to the sky, letting the snow fall on her face.

A moment later they were in the church brushing off the snow and laughing. Brie's nose was a bright pink beneath her sparkling eyes. Jesse took their coats and hung them in the small room off the main hallway, and then they found a seat in the sanctuary.

He preferred to sit near the front, but he knew it made a lot of people uncomfortable, so he chose a seat near the middle. Jesse let Brie slide in first, and he sat on the end. He wanted to be a buffer for her from the people he knew would come and greet them. Jesse loved that he attended a friendly church, but he also remembered his first day and how uncomfortable he felt with everyone coming up to him and introducing themselves.

Sure enough, as soon as they sat down, the people began arriving. With each one, Jesse shook hands first before introducing Brie. If anyone knew that she was Brie Carter, daughter of the billionaire, they kept it to themselves for which Jesse was glad. He was sure the last thing she wanted was more attention drawn to her.

When the people stopped coming and the music started, he felt Brie relax next to him.

BRIE WAS glad when the music started, and the people stopped coming by. Her nerves were already on edge and meeting a ton of new people just frazzled them more. When the songs ended, the pastor took the stage. Brie wasn't sure what she expected, but she hadn't pictured the thin man with a receding hairline. He wasn't dressed in a suit and tie but a simple button-down shirt and slacks.

When he opened his mouth, his voice was calm and even though he spoke on a tough topic, he kept an even keel throughout. Brie was transfixed by the sermon as the pastor spoke on loving the people of the world but not being a part of it.

"We are in tough times right now. The world is telling us one thing while the Bible tells us another, and unfortunately some who have spoken out in hate have given Christians a bad name. Neither God nor Jesus told us to hate. In fact, the Bible says we are not to judge. That is God's place. We are to hold other believers accountable if we know they are sinning to help them see the error of their ways, so they can come back to Jesus. Even then, we are to do it with love. If they repent and come back, we are to forgive them as Jesus forgives them. None of us are perfect and we all need forgiveness.

"As for the world, and by this, I mean those who do not profess to follow Jesus, we are to love the people, so they see the light of Jesus within us and ask why we are different. Does this mean we enable and endorse things we know are against what God would want? Not at all but remember that God does not weigh sin. God says we are to be in the world but not of the world. So, instead of focusing on others' sins, focus instead on being the light of Jesus. And instead of spouting hateful words, use your mouths to pray. This is not only what God commands us, but it will present an example for the world they cannot attack."

Brie was not one for politics, but she was not ignorant to the vitriol in the world. She had never heard someone speak on simply showing love and praying. Nor had she really understood what acting like Jesus meant. Was that why Jesse seemed so different to her?

She posed that very question to him on the way back to her apartment. "Are you so different because of Jesus?"

Jesse glanced over at her briefly before returning his attention to the road. "What do you mean different?"

Brie bit her lip as she thought. "I don't know. You're unlike everyone I've known. You don't seem to care about the latest trends or getting into the hottest parties."

Jesse smiled. "Well, that's probably a lot of regular people who aren't billionaires. We don't get invited to those parties often."

"Okay, but there's also the thing with the kids at the hospital. I know a lot of people who have the money to do what you do, and they don't."

"I do try to live the way Jesus would want me to live. As the pastor said, I am not perfect, but I try to be an example for others. And when I mess up, I know that God is faithful and just and will forgive my sins if I confess them and repent. I also try to admit when I'm wrong. For example, I thought when I first met you that you were just a spoiled rich girl like a lot of other wealthy people I've known. I judged you before knowing you, and that was wrong. I'm sorry."

Brie bit back a smile and shook her head. "No, you were right. I was a spoiled rich girl, but this week, I've started to see things differently. I even went to a party last night and left early. I didn't know why but just felt like I didn't belong."

"I think you could do amazing things if you put your energy toward helping others. With your money and influence, you could really make a difference."

"Yeah, I've been thinking about that. I'm going to ask my father if he'll help if I go back to school. I never knew what I wanted to do, but after losing my mom and seeing those kids, I think I want to look into nutrition. I've heard that some foods can help with diseases, and I really want to help those kids."

Jesse flashed her another grin, one that lit his face up from ear to ear and displayed a tiny dimple in his cheek she hadn't noticed before. He was no Kade Sinclair, but he was handsome in his own way. "I believe you would be a wonderful nutritionist or dietician."

His words warmed Brie's heart in a way she hadn't felt in a long time. When they pulled up to her apartment, she waited for him to open her door before stepping out of the truck. There was just something about him opening her door that made her feel special.

"I'm really glad you came to church with me this morning," he said when they reached her door.

"I'm glad I came too. It was a nice place, and if you're open to it, I'd like to go again."

"I'd love it if you would come again." He grabbed her hands, sending a funny sensation up her arms, and folded them against his heart. "I'm glad Brendan asked me to give you a chance."

"Me too." Her voice was quiet as she looked up at him. Was he going to kiss her this time? His eyes held her gaze and then dropped to her lips. Ever so slowly his face lowered to hers, and his lips touched hers. They were soft and sweet but sent a heat pulsing through her body. All too quickly, he pulled back, and she opened her eyes.

"Would you like to go ice skating tomorrow?"

Brie blinked at him. She hadn't been expecting that

question, but she would not pass up any time with Jesse. "I'd love to."

"Wonderful," he tucked a strand of hair behind her ears, sending another jolt of electricity down her spine, "as long as nothing catastrophic happens tomorrow, I should be off by six pm."

"I should be off by four, so that will work out perfectly."

He held her gaze another moment before planting another quick kiss and then walking away. On cloud nine, Brie walked into her apartment. She couldn't remember the last time she had felt like this.

She dropped her purse and hung up her coat before dialing her father's number. Now that she had told Jesse of her plan, she just needed to inform her father. "Hey, Dad, when you get a chance can I come see you or can you stop by my apartment? I have a proposition I want to discuss with you."

"How about we meet for dinner tonight?" her father suggested. "I have a meeting to finish here, but I could meet you at five."

"It's a date." Brie smiled as she hung up. She just hoped her father would be as excited about this as she was.

"DAD, I want to go back to school," Brie said as they sat

down at a table in the far back of the restaurant. It was her dad's personal table as far as she could figure as it was the same one they ate at every time they came to this restaurant.

His eyebrow arched, and he leaned back and folded his arms across his chest. "I see. And what do you think you would like to study this time? Shopping? Jewelry making?"

Brie knew she deserved that; she had been too flighty in the past, but she needed to let him know this time really was different. "No, Dad, I want to go to school to study nutrition."

"Why? You don't need to go on a diet, Brie. You look fine just the way you are."

Brie took a deep breath. She had practiced what she was going to say at her apartment, but she hoped her father would listen. "No, it's not about me. I met a guy this last week…"

He leaned forward interrupting her, "Oh, so this is about a guy."

"No, Dad, if you would just listen. I met this guy who is unlike anyone I've met before, and he took me to the children's hospital. He delivers toys to the kids there when he can. I almost couldn't go in because of what happened to mom, but I'm glad I did. You should have seen these kids' faces when they saw Jesse. I'd like to do something like he does, some donation or something, but it got me thinking too. I really want to study nutrition and see if I can use food to help cure diseases like cancer."

"Brie, I'm not sure food can cure cancer."

"Dad, I've done research. They are finding that certain foods and certain diets can help slow diseases and even reverse their effects. I want to help. I could work at the hospital or maybe a clinic and help people."

Her father leaned back again and narrowed his eyes at her. "Where is this coming from, Brie? I love you, but you haven't thought much about anyone but yourself for years."

Brie sighed and dropped her eyes to the table. "I know, Dad, but then I met Jesse and you made me get a job. I saw how the other half lives, and I don't want to work at the coffee place for the rest of my life. This would allow me to get a better paying job. One I love. And isn't that what you always said? That I should do something I love?"

Her father chuckled and ran a hand across his strong chin. Brie had the same chin though hers thankfully was a little smaller and more feminine looking. "I'll help you pay for college on two conditions."

"What are they?" Brie clasped her hands together and bit the inside of her lip to keep her enthusiasm from bubbling out before she heard the conditions.

"One, I want you to keep working at the coffee shop. I know it's not your dream job, but it will give you a resume which you'll need when you get out of college."

Brie sighed, but she had expected he would want her to continue working. And while being a barista wasn't that fantastic, the hours weren't bad and would allow her to go to school. Plus, he hadn't stipulated a minimum number of hours she needed to work each week. "Okay, what's the second condition?"

"I'd like to meet this man who has so greatly affected my daughter."

Brie's face broke into a grin. That one would be easy to comply with. "I'll be happy to introduce you, but I have to warn you, he's SWAT, so his schedule is a little challenging."

"We will make it work."

Their food arrived then, and the two enjoyed a wonderful meal and the nicest conversation Brie could remember having with her father in a long time.

10

Jesse arrived at Brie's apartment at six pm on the dot. Thankfully, there had been no calls at work, and the men had been able to relax a little. Jesse had even gotten to spend a little time with Bugsy before driving to Brie's. A rarity in his job.

He often felt sorry for the dog. Jesse had gotten him when he first moved to New York as he had wanted company. After joining SWAT, his time had dwindled, and Bugsy spent a lot of time alone. He paid for a dog walker a few days a week, but he knew it wasn't the same. Still, he couldn't bear the thought of giving up Bugsy. The dog was still his companion when he was home, and Jesse wasn't sure he would stay in SWAT forever.

Jesse pressed the doorbell and a moment later, Brie opened the door. Her soft pink sweater brought out a sparkle in her blue eyes and matched the color of her lip gloss.

"You are punctual, aren't you?" Brie asked with a laugh.

Jesse smiled back. He liked her laugh. It reminded him of the triangle he was forced to play in third grade. Back then, everyone took turns on different instruments. Jesse loved the xylophones and the drums, but he had never enjoyed playing the triangle. It just hadn't seemed very important. However, he had always loved the sound, and Brie's laugh was light and tinkly like the triangle.

"I try. It's sort of a requirement for the job. You ready?"

"I am, but I have to warn you, I'm pretty good at skating. It was the one sport my father put me in that I actually enjoyed until it became too much work." She rolled her eyes and shook her head. "I really was spoiled."

"Well, I grew up in the mountains of Montana. Believe me, I had plenty of practice skating. In fact, I was on our ice hockey team in high school." He had played a lot of sports in high school, but boxing and hockey had been his favorites.

"Game on then." She grabbed a bag and closed the door behind her. Jesse took her free hand, enjoying the feel of her smaller hand in his and led the way to the elevator.

Twenty minutes later, they arrived at the rink. He had hoped if they came right around dinner time that it wouldn't be crowded, but it seemed several other couples had the same idea. They had to wait for a bench to clear before they could sit and lace up their skates.

Jesse felt like a stalker as they waited between two benches. When the couple to the left stood, he and Brie swooped in and secured the bench, giggling like school kids who were breaking the rules. They took off their shoes and laced up their skates, then found a place to leave their street shoes.

Jesse took her hand as they stepped onto the ice. It took him a minute to reacquaint his legs to the feel of ice beneath them, but soon it came flooding back. Brie must have had the same issue as she clung to his arm the first lap around, but by the second, she was skating confidently. A few times, she even let go to skate ahead of him and perform a fancy spin or jump. He smiled as he watched her. With her blond hair flying out around her, she looked like an angel, and Jesse felt himself falling for her.

BRIE LAUGHED as she spun and glanced back at Jesse. There was something about him that she found endearing. So much so that she knew she needed to tell him about the bet. But she didn't want to ruin the evening. Surely, it could wait a little longer.

She skated back to him and grabbed his hand again.

Her nose was cold from the chilly air, and she knew her cheeks were flushed pink as well. "I'm hungry. Do you want to get a hot dog? I know of a great stand around here."

"A hot dog?" He chuckled. "I kind of thought you'd be…" he paused as if searching for the right words.

"A food snob?" she asked.

A pink blush colored his cheeks and she knew that was exactly what he had been thinking. "I wasn't going to say it like that, more like a refined palette."

"I have one of those," she said as they skated back to where they had placed their shoes, "but I also grew up with just my dad for most of my life. He used to take me to ball games and buy me hot dogs."

Jesse's eyes lit up. "Oh yeah, who's your favorite team?"

"Well, I've always been partial to football, so I guess the Patriots."

Jesse tsked and shook his head. "You live in New York and you aren't a Giants fan? I don't know if we can still be friends."

Brie swatted his arm though she knew he was kidding. He caught her hand and pulled her to his chest. Brie's breath stilled, and she smiled up at him. She liked the soft copper stubble that colored his cheeks and the gold flecks in his hazel eyes. His gaze held hers just a moment before he leaned down and kissed her. Heat flared across her lips and traveled through her body. She'd never felt such a connection with anyone before.

"Okay, I guess we can still be friends," Jesse said when he pulled back. The teasing glint still sparkled in his eyes.

"Oh good, so glad you agree." The two took their shoes to an empty bench and changed back into their regular footwear. Then Brie led the way out of the rink and to one of her favorite street vendors.

Hot dogs were not her normal fare as they weren't very healthy, but every once in a while, she just got a craving for a loaded dog. She recognized her favorite vendor as they approached. "Hey, Charlie, how's business been?"

"Not too bad, you know how it goes." Charlie had a thick New York accent and always wore a derby atop his head.

"Well, how about a little more business? Do you have a loaded hot dog for my friend Jesse and I?"

"Of course, anything for you, Ms. Brie." He loaded up two hot dogs and handed them over in exchange for the money Brie pulled out.

"I could have bought my own dog," Jesse whispered as they wandered over to a nearby table.

"I know, but it was my treat. You've been so sweet to me."

"I'm just glad the guys convinced me to give you a chance. I honestly thought it had to be a joke that you liked me. I'm not typically the ones girls flock over. That's usually Brendan."

Brie's eyes dropped to her lap. There was no way she could tell him about the bet now. Even worse, she'd have to keep Ariel away from Jesse or her friend might let it slip that she too had wanted Brendan at first.

"Well, I'm glad you gave me a chance too."

A comfortable silence fell between them as they finished their hot dogs, and then they walked back to Jesse's truck.

"Can I show you something?" he asked as he opened the door for her.

"Sure. I'd like that." The sun had set while they were skating, and only tiny streaks of pink still lit the sky at the horizon. Brie was sure the stars were beginning to emerge, but with all the lights in the city, it was impossible to see them.

She buckled her seatbelt as he climbed in the driver's side and started the truck. He headed away from the city lights and she wondered where they were going.

Half an hour later, they were on the outskirts of the city, away from all the lights. Brie had never seen it so dark. Jesse pulled the truck over and opened her door.

"What are we doing out here?" Brie hoped she hadn't misjudged him now that she was in the middle of nowhere in the dark with him.

"I thought you might like to see some stars. It's not quite the same way I grew up seeing them in Montana, but it's pretty close." He lowered the tailgate to the truck and then grabbed a blanket from the cab and spread it out in the truck bed. He dropped the second blanket in the bed and held out his hand to her. "Come on."

She took it and climbed into the bed beside him. He propped up some rope to make a makeshift pillow and opened his arm. Brie curled up against his chest and looked up. Then she gasped. The stars lit up the sky like tiny diamonds. "It's so beautiful. Is this how it looked in Montana?

Jesse chuckled. "Not quite. It was even more impressive back where I grew up. There were fewer lights around."

"That must have been an amazing sight."

"It was, but not as beautiful as you." He brushed her hair behind her ear and placed his lips on hers. Brie's pulse doubled, and a reckless feeling flooded her veins. Before anything more could happen, Jesse pulled back.

"Sorry, I can't let it go any further. I want to, but I want to be married first, the way God intended it."

Brie blinked. "You mean you've never…" she didn't know how to finish the statement without a serious blush taking over.

"I didn't say that. I wasn't always a Christ follower and I made a lot of mistakes when I was younger. I'm trying to make fewer now."

Brie thought about that. She hadn't considered her past a mistake, but the more she revisited it, the more it made sense. After her last relationship ended, she had felt used and had wished she hadn't let it get as far as she had. Maybe there was something to waiting until there was a commitment.

"I admire that about you." She snuggled into his arms once again. "Most guys I've known have only been after the prize."

He squeezed her shoulder. "Don't get me wrong. I'm after the prize. I just want the forever one rather than the short-term one."

Brie smiled and shook her head slightly. If Jesus was what made Jesse so different, she was beginning to think she wanted Him too.

11

"What do you mean you can't go out? It's been three weeks, Brie. Three weeks since we've hung out."

Brie sighed and pinched her nose. She knew she hadn't been spending as much time with Ariel, but she had gotten accepted into the nutrition program at the local college and was spending a few nights a week in class. Brie generally spent the other evenings with Jesse when he was off work or researching when he wasn't. And work filled her days.

Besides, after everything that had happened in the last three weeks, she didn't feel she had as much in common with Ariel any more. Her father still hadn't reinstated her credit cards so shopping trips were out of the question. And honestly, she didn't feel the need to go shopping anyway. She felt the need to purge some of her items. She worked nearly every morning, something Ariel had no concept of, and she had committed her life to Christ, so parties no longer held any meaning for her.

"I know, Ariel, and I'm so sorry, but I've got work and school and Jesse…"

"I knew this was about Jesse," Ariel seethed, cutting her off. "I should never have suggested the bet. I thought you would have a little fun, but he's changed you. Now, you're no fun at all."

"I'm fun. Just in a different way. Look, you want to hang out with me? Come to church with me tomorrow." Brie glanced at her watch. She was going to have to cut this short as her break was almost over.

"Church? Are you listening to yourself? Who are you?"

"Ariel, I have to get back to work, but I would like to see you. I get off at four if you want to get together before you go out tonight."

"Yeah, we'll see." The phone went dead in Brie's ear, and she shook her head and pushed the phone back in her pocket.

"Everything okay?" Matt asked as he entered the break room.

"Yeah, just my friend. She doesn't like the changes I've made recently."

"Well, I have to say you have proved a model employee. I was a little worried when I first hired you, but you have definitely improved since you've been here."

"Thank you, Matt. I appreciate you giving me a chance. I better get back to work now. Break's over." She flashed a small wave and headed back to the counter. Matt was nice, but as they were about the same age, she didn't want to give him any suggestion she might be interested.

As she took her position behind the counter again, Brie thought about her conversation with Ariel. Was she going to lose her best friend?

JESSE WHISTLED as he packed up his gear for the night. It had been another nice day with no crazy calls and no shots fired at them.

"You seem pretty happy. Things going well with Brie then?"

Jesse turned to Brendan who had entered the locker room behind him. "Yes, things are going better than I could have hoped. I'm glad you convinced me to give her a shot."

Brendan's face fell, and he rubbed his chin. "Yeah, don't go thanking me just yet. Her friend Ariel is at the front desk asking to talk to you."

"Me? What for?" Jesse had heard Brie talk about Ariel, but he'd never met her. What on earth could she want to talk to him about?

Brendan shrugged. "I'd rather she tell you herself."

Trepidation seized Jesse as he slung his bag over his shoulder and headed for the front door. Was something wrong with Brie? Had she decided he wasn't rich enough for her? That seemed unlikely, but it was a fear he couldn't get out of his head.

He pushed open the door to the foyer, and a dark-haired girl looked up. She was thin and pretty, and she oozed money. Jesse did not miss her designer shoes as she stood and clacked his direction nor was he oblivious to the expensive bag slung over her shoulder.

"Ariel? I'm Jesse. What can I do for you?" He extended his hand towards her, but she ignored it.

"I know who you are, but I have some information you don't know. Brie is playing you. See, we made a bet. She was bored and wanted to have a little fun, so I bet her she couldn't get a guy to propose to her after a month. You were the target, and my brother Kade was the prize. If she could get you to propose, I'd set her up on a date with my brother."

Anger and disbelief filled Jesse, and a vice-grip feeling squeezed his heart. Could Brie do such a thing? He had found it odd she would want him over Brendan or Carter, but he didn't think she would do such a thing. Had she been pretending the last few weeks then? "Why are you telling me this now?"

"Because I want my friend back. She spends all her free time with you. I guess she is having a hard time convincing you to propose. So, I don't care about the bet anymore. I'll set her up with Kade whether or not you propose. At least then I'll see her more." She tilted her head at him as if making sure her words were sinking in.

Jesse shook his head, but he couldn't find the words.

"You couldn't honestly believe she'd want a commoner. Brie comes from money, and you could never support her the way she's used to, but Kade is a famous actor. He has the money to support her lifestyle."

"I see. Well, thank you for letting me know." Jesse felt deflated. He had opened his heart to Brie even after his own hesitations. He should have known to trust his gut.

"You're welcome." She flashed a smile, but to Jesse it seemed more malicious than endearing.

As he watched her leave, he wondered what to do about Brie. He was supposed to meet her tonight, but he no longer felt the desire. However, he also didn't want to just stand her up. No matter what she'd done, no one deserved that.

With a heavy heart, he trudged to his truck. Why did he seem to have such rotten luck with women? Was he just destined to remain single? As he pulled out of the parking lot, he decided to stop at Java Hut and tell her in person he was calling their date off that night. He didn't really want to affect her work, but it was the best solution he could think of, and he knew she would be getting off soon.

He pulled into the parking lot right at four. Brie should be heading out any minute. He took a deep breath as he thought of what to say to her. Before the thoughts settled in his head, the door opened, and she appeared. She hadn't been expecting him, and he could see the surprise register on her face as she spotted his truck. Being bright blue, it didn't blend in easily.

A smile lit her face and she hurried his direction. Jesse turned off the engine and stepped out to meet her.

"Hey, I wasn't expecting to see you here."

Jesse folded his arms. "I wasn't expecting to come here, but I got a visit today from a friend of yours."

Confusion clouded Brie's eyes, and she shook her head. "What do you mean? Why do you sound angry?"

Jesse scoffed. "I sound angry because your friend told me these last three weeks have meant nothing. That you pursued me to win a bet, so you could date some movie star."

Brie's hand flew to her mouth and her blue eyes widened. He wanted to see more confusion in her gaze, but there was a sick realization that shone through.

"How could you do that, Brie? People's emotions aren't toys. I thought you were different."

"I am. I... I did make that bet with Ariel, but then I got to know you, and I fell for you, Jesse. You have to believe me." Brie reached out to grab his arm, but he pulled it away.

"Believe you? You've been lying to me since we met."

Tears flooded Brie's eyes, and she shook her head. "I haven't been lying to you. I may have pursued you because of that bet, but I kept seeing you because I liked you."

"But not more than this movie star? Were you really going to dump me the moment I proposed to you?"

"No, the more I got to know you, the less I wanted Kade. He's arrogant and dismissive, and he never paid attention to me. I bet Ariel didn't tell you I called the bet off, did she?"

Jesse blinked but said nothing. Ariel hadn't mentioned that fact, but did it really matter?

"Within the first week, I told her I didn't want to do that to you. You changed me. This job changed me. Please, Jesse, I'm not the same girl anymore."

"I don't know, Brie, I need some time to think." Jesse ran a hand across his beard and tried not to crumble at Brie's dejected expression.

Brie's lips folded into a tight line and she nodded. She looked like her tears would win any moment, and he didn't want to see that. It might cause him to change his mind, and he really needed to think through everything before he made a decision.

"A few days, just give me a few days," he said and then without waiting for a reply, he climbed in his truck and drove off.

As Brie watched him drive away, pain like she'd never

felt before blanketed her. She walked over to a nearby bench and sat down, letting the tears fall. Why had she ever taken that bet? And how was she going to convince Jesse that she cared about him?

Suddenly words from a recent sermon popped in her head. "God whispers in our pleasures, He speaks in our conscience, but He shouts in our pain." Brie closed her eyes and opened her heart. "Lord, please tell me what to do. I don't want to lose Jesse, but even more I don't want to do anything that would cause him to stumble. Help me to know your will."

Brie sat there another few minutes just waiting and listening. Though no clear voice spoke to her, a sense of peace descended, and Brie knew it would just be a matter of time before she would be able to discern His will.

12

Brie looked around the room and smiled. She couldn't believe she had pulled this off in a week. Of course, her father's connections helped. He had made sure several wealthy friends would be in attendance, but the rest had been up to Brie.

She had secured the venue and the items for the auction. Quite a few had come from her own closet. Items she had purchased but never worn, but she had secured a few art pieces and expensive jewelry as well. Brie owed a lot of people favors now, but it would be worth it if Jesse showed up.

That was the only hitch in her plan. He still wasn't talking to her, so she'd planned a different way to invite him. One she hoped his friends would go along with. Even if they got him there though, that was only half the battle. Then she had to convince him she was serious.

"Ms. Carter, do you have a moment to go over the menu for tonight?"

Brie turned to the older gentleman who was heading up the catering and nodded. "Of course, Pierre." She followed him into the kitchen where he had plates lined up across the counter.

"I thought for an appetizer we would start with a glazed fig topped with mascarpone and wrapped with prosciutto." He gestured to a small bite sized square. Brie could see just the hint of the fig and the mascarpone sticking out of the end. She picked it up and took a bite nodding at the delicate flavors that ignited in her mouth.

"This is wonderful. What's next?"

"Next we have a Salade Nicoise."

Brie took a bite of the colorful salad and gave her approval to it as well.

"For the main course, we will have Pappardelle with Sea Urchin and Cauliflower."

The dish wasn't as colorful as the salad, but the flavors were all there.

"And finally, for dessert, we have Mocha Pots de Creme."

Brie smiled at the tiny cups filled with chocolate. She dipped the tiny spoon in and savored the taste. It took great effort to return the spoon and not eat the entire dessert. "This is fantastic, Pierre. They will love everything."

He nodded. "I am so glad you approve. We will have everything ready to be served at six, no?"

"Yes, the appetizers should start at six. I'd like to be eating the main course at seven so there is plenty of time for the auction."

"As you wish, Ms. Carter. I wish you the best of luck with your endeavor tonight."

Brie thanked him before heading out of the kitchen. She would need luck, but she'd need much more than that. A miracle was more like it.

"WHAT'S GOING on with you, man? You have been quieter and moodier than normal." Patrick shut the door to the office and turned to face Jesse.

Jesse sighed as he regarded the team leader and tried to decide how much to tell him. He didn't want to admit a girl was messing up his game, but he needed to assure Patrick he could still do his job. The fact that Patrick had called this meeting in his office told Jesse that Patrick needed some reassurance.

He jammed his hands in his pockets and took a deep breath. "It's Brie. I found out she only pursued me because of a bet."

Patrick leaned back against his desk and crossed his arms. "That doesn't sound like the girl I've gotten to know." Patrick hadn't been around Brie all that often, but she had stopped in a few times over the last couple of weeks with lunch or dinner for the guys. "Are you sure there isn't more to the story?"

Jesse shrugged and plopped down in one of the open chairs. "She said she called it off the first week when she started to fall for me, but I don't know, how can I be with a girl who lied to me?"

"I'm not saying she was right, but she wasn't exactly lying to you. She just didn't offer up the information, and this is probably why. She probably thought if she told you that she would lose you."

"Yeah, but, how do I trust her going forward? I'll always wonder if her feelings are real."

"Don't they teach you at that church of yours about forgiveness? It sounds like Brie made a mistake, and she is asking you for forgiveness."

"Or else she made up the part about calling off the bet, and as soon as I propose, she'll dump me."

Patrick's brow inched up creating tiny creases across his forehead. "Were you going to propose?"

"Not yet, but I was falling for this one, Patrick. She was so different from what I had thought she was."

"I think she still is. Yes, she made a mistake making a bet like that, but look at it this way, if she hadn't you two might never have met."

Jesse leaned back in the chair and ran his hand across his stubbled chin. He hadn't thought about it that way. He believed God put people in his path for a purpose. Maybe his purpose had been to ground Brie and hers had been to get him to open up again. Still, that didn't make trusting her any easier. He was about to say so when the phone on Patrick's desk rang.

Patrick held up a finger and circled the desk to answer the phone. "Sergeant Hughes." There was a pause and his eyes flicked to Jesse before returning to the phone. "Yes, he's here. Hold on." Patrick punched the hold button on the phone and faced Jesse. "You have anything going on tonight?"

Jesse shook his head. Now that he was no longer seeing Brie, his evenings were empty once again.

"Yes sir. We'll be there." Patrick hung up the phone and stared at it a moment. "That was Mark Avery, head of the Children's Hospital. I guess you are being recognized at some banquet tonight, and we're all invited."

"What? I don't know anything about a banquet."

"Yeah, he apologized for the late notice. Said it was set up out of the blue by a generous donor. Guess we better go tell the guys to dust off their dress uniforms."

Jesse nodded but his mind was a million miles away. What was this surprise banquet? Would he have to give a speech? He hated giving speeches as he'd never been good at it, and this was even more nerve wracking as he had no idea what it would be about.

"All right guys, listen up. Jesse here is a guest of honor at a banquet tonight, and we have all been invited. So, go home, clean up, and be back here at seventeen hundred in your dress uniforms." He looked to Carter. "Spotless and pressed."

Carter balked. "What are you looking at me for? I am always spotless and pressed."

"If you have a wife and can find a sitter, your wife is also invited. If you are single, do not bring a date."

"What? How is that fair?" Brendan argued. "I finally get invited some place fancy, and I can't even show off?"

"I'm sorry, those were the stipulations," Patrick said.

Jared laughed and clapped a hand on Brendan's shoulder. "Guess the old ball and chain isn't so bad after all, huh?"

Brendan returned a jab and Jesse took the opportunity to slip out and grab his things. He didn't want any of the guys asking him questions when he had so many himself. And no answers.

JESSE ARRIVED BACK at the station with five minutes to spare. He felt stiff in his dress uniform. This would be his first time wearing it.

"Well, don't you look nice," Penny said as he entered.

"Thank you. I feel a little like a wooden soldier."

"You should have stretched it out more like I did with mine," Brendan said as he entered the foyer. "I put mine on once a week just to see how good I look."

"Hah, you probably put it on every day," Carter said.

He had entered just behind Brendan. Patrick showed up next minus his wife due to her very pregnant state, but Cam and Jared both entered with their wives on their arms.

"We all here then?" Patrick asked looking around the room. "Good, you all look nice, and our ride should be here," he looked out the front door, "right now."

Jesse turned to see a black stretch limo in front of the station.

Brendan let out a low whistle. "Wow, we get to ride in style."

"Hey, what's with the limo?" Jesse asked Patrick as the rest of the group filed out.

Patrick shook his head. "Just part of the package. You've made quite an impression on someone."

So, it would seem. The questions Jesse had was who? Who had he impressed so much that all of this would be offered to him? He climbed in the limo curious as to what the next few hours would hold.

13

Brie peeked out at the crowd and took a deep breath. She was not a public speaker by nature. Instagram and Facebook videos were about as close as she got, but tonight was important for many reasons. Not only would it be her opportunity to connect with Jesse again, she hoped, but it would also be an opportunity to raise a lot of money and awareness for the Children's hospital.

"If you're ready, Ms. Carter, they are ready for you." Nancy, the sound coordinator, nodded at her. She held a clipboard in her hand, and a mic and earpiece extended from the right side of her face, so she could give directions to the lighting and sound crew.

Brie closed her eyes and whispered a quick prayer and then she stepped up to the microphone. Her eyes scanned the crowd for just a moment, and she smiled when she saw Jesse. She could see the confusion in his eyes. "Thank you all for coming. We are here tonight for two reasons. One, to honor a wonderful man I have gotten to know who has a love for these children. And two, to raise money for some wonderful children. I'd like to show you a video of some of these kids as they are too sick to join us in person. Then I'll share a little about the amazing man I met."

Brie stepped back and watched the video play. She had gone into the Children's hospital a few days prior with a friend who was a videographer and filmed the children after getting permission from their parents. Some shots were of the kids playing, but a few brave souls had agreed to speak on film. They spoke of their illness and how hard it was to be stuck in the hospital, and they spoke of Jesse and how much joy he brought every time he showed up.

When the video ended, Brie surveyed the crowd. Tears glistened in many eyes across the room. It was moving to see that so many people had a soft side. "A few weeks ago, I thought having the newest purse or pair of shoes was the only thing that mattered. I had a closet full of things I hadn't even worn, but then I met this amazing man. He introduced me to these kids and my view began to change. I saw a man who was so giving of his time and his money, and it made me want to be better. I would like to introduce that man to you. Jesse Calhoun, will you come up here?"

All eyes turned to the SWAT table as Jesse stood. Brie

could tell he was uncomfortable, but she also knew the crowd would relate to him. As soon as he joined her at the mic, she turned back to the crowd. "This is Jesse Calhoun. He is a member of New York's SWAT team. More importantly, he is a hero to these children. When he has time, he delivers toys to these kids, and tonight I would like for us to help him. We are going to have an auction in a minute, and all the proceeds are going to this hospital. Even if you don't find anything you would like to buy, I hope you will still donate. These amazing kids are the sweetest ones you will ever meet. They don't ask for anything other than healing, but they find joy in those little things. And this is something we can do for them. So, without further ado, I'm going to ask Robin, our auctioneer, to get this started.

The crowd clapped, and Brie smiled and took Jesse's hand and led him off the stage as Robin took the stage.

"You planned all of this?" he asked as they entered the wing.

"I did. When you left the other day, I was heartbroken, but I finally understood what you meant about needing God. He was there for me when I was at my lowest, and when I prayed for a way to show you that I cared, this came to mind. I know it isn't that personal-"

"It's perfect," he said cutting her off and taking her hand. "Brie, I'm sorry I doubted you. I have hurt in my past that I'm still dealing with, and a friend reminded me that we all make mistakes."

"It's okay, Jesse. I would have doubted me too, but I

meant what I said out there. You have changed me. Well, you and God. I would say I'm sorry I ever took that bet, but I'm not really because if I hadn't, I would never have talked to you. I would have kept living my empty life searching for something I never would have found there."

Jesse smiled, and his hand cupped her face. Brie leaned into it and placed her hand on his enjoying the touch she had been missing for a moment. "We better get back out there before they send a search party for us."

"All right," Jesse said, but the desire remained in his eyes.

Brie led the way back to the floor, and they joined the rest of the SWAT team at the table.

JESSE GRABBED Brie's hand under the table. He still couldn't believe she had put all this together. There were so many items to bid on and the crowd seemed especially generous after watching the video she had put together. When the auction ended, she had raised over a million dollars for the children.

"I have one more gift for you," she said after they had said goodbye to his friends. They had ridden back to the station in the limo and were now standing at his truck.

"Another gift? Brie, you have given me so much

already. The children are so lucky to have you as a friend."

"I know, but I wanted to give you something just for you." She opened her purse and pulled out two rectangular tickets.

Jesse took them, and his eyes widened. "Tickets to the Superbowl? Brie, I can't."

She smiled and touched his arm. "You can, and you will. I had to promise a lot of favors to get these tickets."

"Nothing too awful I hope."

"I have no idea," she said with a laugh, "but whatever they are, it will be worth it. You are worth it." She placed a hand on his chest, and Jesse wrapped his arms around her waist.

"Well, thank you. I know your team isn't playing, but I hope you'll accompany me to the game. I can't imagine anyone I'd rather take."

"I'd be honored." She moved her hands to meet behind his neck and pulled gently. Jesse was only too happy to comply, and he lowered his face until his lips touched hers.

14

SIX MONTHS LATER

"Do you think she'll like it?" Jesse opened the box to show Brendan the diamond ring he had picked out. The gold ring wasn't ostentatious, but he hoped she would like it anyway. He had chosen a one-carat diamond encircled with smaller heart-shaped diamonds, but he still worried the piece would be smaller than she wanted.

"Dude, she loves you. The ring is perfect, and she will love it. I can't believe you are going to pop the question though. Then Carter and I will be the only ones living the single life."

Jesse closed the box and put it back in his pocket. "You could join us, you know? Find a good woman and settle down."

Brendan nodded. "Maybe one day, but I'm not ready yet."

Jesse nodded. He had seen too many couples get married before they were ready and end up divorcing within five years.

"Where are you proposing?" Brendan asked.

"It might sound silly, but I'm planning on proposing at the hospital. It was sort of our first date, and I thought the kids being there would make it extra special."

Brendan clapped Jesse on the shoulder. "I think that will be perfect."

Jesse hoped so. He had been saving for the ring for months and trying to plan the perfect proposal for almost that long.

"WHERE ARE WE GOING?" Brie asked as he held open the door for her. He had told her to dress casually, but nothing else.

He smiled and the dimple she loved appeared in his cheek. "It's a surprise, but I hope you'll love it."

"I'm sure I will." She took his hand after he started the truck and pulled into traffic and he squeezed back.

Half an hour later, her heart soared as they pulled into the children's hospital parking lot. "We brought more gifts?"

"We did. There's been an influx of donations ever since your banquet. You made quite the impression."

"I think you had more to do with it than I did," Brie

said with a smile, "but I'm glad. I think more people could help those in need, and we could certainly use more kindness in this world."

"I couldn't agree more." He parked the truck and then came around to open her door. They grabbed the bags from the bed of the truck and made their way into the hospital. After waving to the nurse on duty, they headed upstairs to the children's area.

Linda greeted them again and Brie wondered if the woman ever had a day off. "Officer Calhoun, Brie, it's so good to see you. We can't thank you enough for all you've done for the children. They will be so happy to see you."

"Thank you, Linda. In fact, I have a favor to ask of you and them. Can you stay with Brie for a minute?"

"Of course." Linda's confusion mirrored Brie's own. What was he doing?

Jesse smiled and trotted off to the play area where a large group of kids were sure to be congregated.

"Do you know what this is about?" Brie asked the nurse.

"Don't have a clue. I thought you must be in on it."

A moment later, Jesse appeared with a group of kids. Some Brie recognized, and others were new to her. It saddened her, a little, that this place seemed to have a rotation of children coming through. Brie wished that kids never had to come here.

It was bittersweet to see Kyla in the group. She had

hoped the girl had gone into remission, but she was still fighting. "Ms. Brie, Mr. Jesse has a question for you."

"He does, does he?" Brie smiled at Kyla before looking up to Jesse, her brow raised in question.

"I do. I know this isn't the most romantic place, but as it was our first date and it has a special meaning to us, I thought it would do, so Brie Elizabeth Carter," he got down on one knee and Brie's heart stopped, "will you marry me?" He opened a small black velvet box to reveal a beautiful diamond ring.

Linda gasped beside her and Kyla smiled. "Will you, Ms. Brie?"

Brie smiled and looked back to Jesse. "Of course I will."

His grin stretched from ear to ear as he took the ring out of the box and slid it on her finger. It was a perfect fit just as Brie knew it would be. Somehow, even though they had started as complete opposites, she and Jesse made a great pair. And she couldn't wait to start the rest of her life with him.

The End!

IT'S NOT QUITE THE END!

Thank you so much for reading *The Billionaire's Impromptu Bet*. It was a joy to write and partly because it was based on my friend Jesse at the gym. He really is a boxer and until ours broke, he was amazing at the speed bag. He taught me a thing or two, but I'm nowhere near as good as he is. Of course, he's not a SWAT officer in real life, but that's where I get to take some liberties. Still, I hope you enjoyed the story. If you did, would you do me a favor? Just click here and leave a review. It doesn't have to be long - just a few words to help other readers know what they're getting.

I'd love to hear from you, not only about this story, but about the characters or stories you'd like read in the future. I'm always looking for new ideas and if I use one of your characters or stories, I'll send you a free ebook and paperback of the book with a special dedication. Write to me at loranahoopes@gmail.com. And if you'd like to see what's coming next, be sure to stop by authorloranahoopes.com

I also have a weekly newsletter that contains sneak peeks, prize opportunities, book deals, and some about my life. I'll even send you the first chapter of my newest (maybe not even released yet) book if you'd like to sign up.

And if you're interested in meeting the rest of the billionaires in the series, be sure to check out The Billionaire's Secret. Turn the page for a sneak peek.

15

THE BILLIONAIRE'S SECRET PREVIEW

Maxwell Banks smiled at the buxom blond across from him. Her name had escaped his memory, but she would make a suitable companion for the night. The image of her long blond hair splayed like gold across his pillow filled his mind, sending his pulse into overdrive. Her yoga instructor body was just calling out for his attention if the tight shirt she was sporting was any indication.

Discreetly, he turned his wrist to check his watch. Fifteen minutes since they finished dinner. Surely that was a long enough segment of small talk. "You want to finish this somewhere more comfortable?" He reached across the table to stroke her hand as he said the words. A little flattery went a long way. He had mastered that art in the last few years.

Her tongue darted out and swiped across her lips, and her teeth bit the bottom one, causing the blood to flow to it and tint it a shade darker. "Um, sure, I guess that would be okay."

Her words were hesitant, and Maxwell knew he would have to turn up his charm. He didn't usually have to work hard to get women to come home with him. With his dark hair, blue eyes, broad shoulders, and chiseled chest his looks alone attracted many. The fact that he came from money attracted the rest. Those were the harder ones to get rid of, the ones after his money. They tended to show up uninvited and blow his phone up all hours of the day.

But this one wasn't looking for a sugar daddy. This one he picked up in yoga class. Yoga was not usually his thing; he preferred lifting and running, but his friend Justin had dared him to try the class, and as the instructor was hot, Maxwell had taken the chance.

He could tell when he entered the large room that she found him attractive as her eyes followed him as he crossed the room to grab a mat. His blue cut-off t-shirt had showed off his muscular arms and brought out his eyes, and his playing dumb had kept her by his side most of the class. Asking for her number had been easy after that. He had simply put on his puppy dog face and emphasized the need for private lessons if he was ever going to improve. She had fallen for it; hook, line, and sinker. Now it was time to seal the deal.

"Great." He whipped out his wallet and placed four twenties on the table. It was more than enough money as she only had salad and water–another perk to taking out weight conscious women. Then he stretched out his hand to her.

"Don't you need to wait for the change?" she asked, glancing around for the waiter.

"No, I believe in big tips." He flashed his best smile, hoping it would soothe some of the hesitation in her voice.

She shook her head in disbelief, but accepted his outstretched hand. He gave it a squeeze for good measure and then led her out of the restaurant and back to his black BMW Z4.

"What about my car? Shouldn't I just follow you?" She glanced around for her car in the full parking lot.

"Don't worry about it. I'll bring you back to your car later." Her smile relaxed as he opened the car door for her, and she slid into the grey leather seat.

After shutting her door, Max walked to the driver's side, folded himself into the driver's seat and turned on the engine. As the air had cooled considerably, he pressed the button for the heated seats before pulling out of the restaurant parking lot.

The girl—he really should remember her name—pulled on her skirt to stretch it back down. It had crept up her leg revealing her smooth, toned thighs underneath.

"Can I turn on some music?"

Max mentally kicked himself. He'd been so distracted with her thighs that he hadn't realized they were driving in silence. Silence was never good. It let them think. "Of course, whatever you'd like."

She punched the buttons on the dial a few times before landing on some newer pop music. Inwardly, he cringed–he was more of a hard rock fan himself, but he knew the payout would be worth it.

Fifteen minutes later, he heard the sharp intake of her breath as he pulled into the driveway of his house. While not a mansion, the 4000-foot ranch home was impressive. The craftsman style boasted three slanted roofs, two chimneys, a grey-brick exterior, and a white wraparound front porch. A small working fountain sat in the middle of the circular drive.

"You live here?" The awe was plain in her voice.

He smiled inside. The deal was almost sealed now. "Yeah, it's a little big for one person, but I hope one day to fill it with a family."

When she turned back to him, he could almost see the stars in her eyes.

He pulled into the three-car garage and parked next to his Harley Davidson. The third bay contained no vehicle. At least not yet. The garage was neat as Max detested messes, and the few tools he owned meticulously lined the shelves along the wall.

Her heels clicked across the cement floor as he led her

to the door into the house. It opened onto a large laundry room with a washer, dryer, and table to fold clothes on. The door from the laundry room led into the hallway. To the left was the kitchen, dining room, and family room. To the right were the bedrooms. Max turned left, leading her to where he had a bottle of wine waiting on the counter. It was yet another tactic he had learned would loosen women up and lower their inhibitions.

The large kitchen was half the size of the first floor of most houses. Stainless steel appliances filled the room, and a marble topped island in a crème color with brown and gold flecks sat predominantly in the middle of the room. A large silver light fixture hung above the island, and a deep sink took up a portion of the space under the light. The island hosted a bottle of red wine and two glasses, and across from the sink four plush barstools covered in black leather lined the island. The cabinets that circled the room were a deep brown, and a large walk-in pantry covered most of the back wall, but it was the wine Max focused on.

"Drink?" he asked as he uncorked the bottle and began pouring the glasses.

"Oh, I don't know if I should. I can't stay too long. I teach an early class tomorrow." The hesitation was creeping back into her voice, and her eyes darted around as if she might bolt. It was time to turn up the charm.

Max pushed his lower lip out in a slight pout. "You

wouldn't make me drink alone, would you? Besides, what will one glass hurt?" The glass he extended to her was half full, and he focused his steely blue eyes on her. Many women had told him that his eyes were what drew them in, and Max knew how to use them to his advantage.

Her eyes flickered back and forth, but returned to his gaze, and he knew he had her. "Okay, maybe just one." Her arm rose and accepted the glass.

"To a wonderful night with a beautiful woman," he said, clinking her glass ever so slightly. A blush spread across her face, and she dropped her eyes to the murky red liquid as she took a sip. Max was about to suggest they retire to the living room, where his leather couch would be more inviting and conducive to his seduction, when the doorbell rang.

A glance at his watch revealed it was nearly ten p.m. No one he knew should be ringing his bell, and it was too late for solicitors. "Make yourself comfortable," he said to her, "I'll be right back."

As his shoes echoed on the hardwood flooring, he cursed the timing of whoever stood on the other side of the door. He had worked hard to get this woman here, and she had proven more skittish than many before her. If he lost her because of this interruption, there would be retribution.

Max was fully prepared to lash into the unfortunate soul on the other side of the door, but when he swung it open, his heart stopped, and his words failed him. The anger sizzled as if doused like a campfire, and he blinked not believing his eyes.

CONTINUE READING The Billionaire's Secret...

Or get the boxed set with all 4 books and save 38%

16

A FREE STORY FOR YOU

ENJOYED THIS STORY? Not ready to quit reading yet? If you sign up for my newsletter, you will receive The Reality Bride's Baby right away as my thank you gift for choosing to hang out with me.

The Reality Bride's Baby

Read on for a taste of The Reality Bride's Baby….

17

THE REALITY BRIDE'S BABY PREVIEW

Laney splashed water on her face and dried it off. She hoped she wasn't getting sick but her stomach had felt funny all morning. Like butterflies flapping around or pancakes being flipped in her stomach. Now dizziness overwhelmed her, but she just needed to make it through the next hour and then she could go home and rest.

It was probably silly that she had wanted to walk. After all, she was almost thirty, but she hadn't walked for her certificate for cosmetology and she wanted to hear her name called, shake the Dean's hand and flip her tassel. Besides, Tyler, Aaron, and Nancy had insisted they wanted to come cheer for her as she received her teaching degree. She just hoped whatever was affecting her stomach would calm down.

"Hey, it's about to start," her friend, Tia, said popping

her head in the bathroom. Tia was studying to be a high school math teacher, but the two had bonded during the program and Laney would miss her after they graduated tonight.

"Right, be right there." Her mouth still felt funny though like that coppery metallic taste that made your mouth produce excess saliva. She usually only had that sensation before she was about to vomit but Laney hoped it didn't mean that today. Tossing her cookies while on stage held zero appeal.

She splashed one more handful of water on her face, patted it dry, took a deep breath and followed Tia out to where the other graduates were lining up.

"Are you okay?" Tia asked. "You look pale."

"Yeah, I don't know what's going on but my stomach doesn't feel right. Maybe I'm just nervous?"

Tia's left eyebrow lifted in a quizzical expression. "Girl, you appeared on a reality dating show and got married on national TV. How could you be nervous walking across a stage?"

Tia had a point but Laney didn't want to accept the fact she might truly be sick. "A TV show is a little different. There were cameras yes but not hundreds of people staring at us."

"All right, graduates, it's time." The voice of the education professor kept Tia from responding. Laney stepped into her place in line and prayed she would make it through the ceremony. *Just through the ceremony, God, please.*

The filled auditorium sent a wave of warmth rolling over Laney as she stepped through the doorway. Or maybe it was oppressive heat. Beads of sweat formulated on her back and one rolled down her spine. Her mouth began to salivate again. She followed the person in front of her down the aisle and to a chair. Sitting didn't stop the craziness in her stomach, but it helped a little, and her dizziness ebbed slightly.

The master of ceremonies stepped up to the podium and tapped the mic lightly. "Welcome friends and graduates. We've worked long and hard but our time has now come to an end." Though he continued, Laney's brain refused to pay attention.

She scanned the crowd hoping to find her husband and friends. It shouldn't have been too hard as Nancy would have baby Sarah with her but Laney saw no sign of a baby or her husband. Perhaps they were too far back. She didn't want to turn in her seat and draw attention to herself. Laney glanced back at the stage but the MC still droned on. She turned her wrist to see her watch. Only ten minutes had passed. How long had they said the ceremony would be again?

"Will you stop fidgeting?" Tia whispered at her.

Right. Focus. Why was she having trouble focusing? She rarely had trouble focusing. Her stomach churned again. Had she eaten? Maybe her stomach was simply hungry because she skipped lunch. No, she had eaten but just a salad. She'd been busy today and hadn't had time for much else. In addition, her clothes had been fitting a little snugger lately, so a salad seemed like a good way to drop a few pounds.

"Edward Coburn."

Her eyes flicked to the stage. Oh good, they were calling names. She wished she could walk off the stage and to her car after getting her diploma but that would look rude. Could she sneak out using the bathroom as an excuse though? It wouldn't even be a fake excuse. She felt the need to splash cool water on her face again. Was she having hot flashes? No, she was too young for that. Probably a fever then. Good thing school had ended for the summer.

"Let's go."

"What?" Laney looked over at Tia who had nudged her in the side.

"It's our turn. Come on." She pointed to the left where the rest of the people in the row were standing and filing toward the stage. Laney shot to her feet eager to catch up with them but the sudden movement sent the room spinning. She grabbed ahold of a chair back to steady herself. When the room stayed still she continued toward the stage but the dizziness remained.

"Jeffrey Hackworth."

The man in front of her stepped up the stairs and Laney grabbed the railing. Just a few more minutes. Then she could make a beeline for the bathroom again. She didn't even care if it seemed rude. It would be better than the alternative.

"Laney Hall."

Laney vaguely registered the cheers and clapping as she forced her feet up the steps. Thank goodness there were only three, but the room began spinning again as soon as she reached the stage. She blinked trying to focus on where to go. The Dean. Yes, he was handing out the diplomas. Her fingers touched the hard black leather bifold and the world went dark.

TYLER'S HEART stopped beating as he watched Laney crumple on the stage. For a moment all he could do was stare as the room gasped and then fell silent. Suddenly, his heart started again and fueled his adrenaline. He pushed past the people in his row and raced toward the front. Before he was halfway there others closer to the stage jumped into action as well.

"Someone call 911."

"Is there a doctor in the room? We need a doctor."

The voices melded together in the pandemonium of the room. Unable to place any except his own, Tyler kept repeating, "That's my wife. Let me through," as he struggled to get past people and to the stage.

By the time he made it to her, Laney's eyes were open

though she was still lying down. Her gaze caught his as he leaned over her. "Laney, are you okay? What happened?"

"I don't know. I think I might be sick. My stomach has been churning and I felt dizzy before we entered but I thought I could make it through the ceremony." Her hands patted around at her sides. "Did I get my degree?"

Tyler shook his head as he took her hand. Of course *that* was what she worried about. Not the dizziness or the fact that she passed out on stage. "I'll make sure you get it," he said.

A few minutes later the paramedics arrived and loaded Laney on a stretcher ignoring her protests.

"I don't need the hospital," she said, "I just needed to lie down and maybe eat a little."

"Just let them do their job," Tyler said as he followed them out. Surely, he could get a ride back to get the car from Nancy or Aaron later.

The short ride to the hospital did not lessen his unease. What was wrong with Laney? Was it serious? It wasn't like her to pass out. Fall? Yes. She had done that quite a few times around him but that was because she was a bit of a klutz. This was entirely different.

The ambulance pulled to a stop in front of the Emergency Room and they wheeled Laney inside.

"This is Laney Hall. Twenty-nine years old. Fainted on stage. Vitals are good. Patient complained of nausea and dizziness."

"Okay. Laney, I'm Dr. Choi. We will take good care of you."

Tyler watched anxiously as they wheeled Laney into a room. He knew she was in good hands but he found it hard to sit in the waiting room and wait for word.

Click here to continue reading The Reality Bride's Baby

THE STORY DOESN'T END!

You've met a few people and fallen in love....

I bet you're wondering how you can meet everyone else.

Star Lake Series:

When Love Returns: The first in the Star Lake series. Presley Hays and Brandon Scott were best friends in High School until Morgan entered their town and stole Brandon's heart. Devastated, Presley takes a scholarship to Le Cordon Bleu, but five years later, she is back in Star Lake after a tough breakup. Brandon thought he'd never return to Star Lake after Morgan left him and his daughter Joy, but when his father needs help, he returns home and finds more than he bargained for. Can Presley and Brandon forget past hurts or will their stubborn natures keep them apart forever?

Once Upon a Star: The second book in the Star Lake

series. Audrey left Star Lake to pursue acting, but after an unplanned pregnancy her jobs and her money dwindled, leaving her no option except to return home and start over. Blake was the quintessential nerd in high school and was never able to tell Audrey how he felt. Now that he's gained confidence and some muscle, will he finally be able to reveal his feelings? Once Upon a Star will take you back to Christmas in Star Lake. Revisit your favorite characters and meet a few ones in this sweet Christmas read.

Love Conquers All: Lanie Perkins Hall never imagined being divorced at thirty. Nor did she imagine falling for an old friend, but when she runs into Azarius Jacobson, she can't deny the attraction. As they begin to spend more time together, Lanie struggles with the fact Azarius keeps his past a secret. What is he hiding? And will she ever be able to get him to open up? Azarius Jacobson has loved Lanie Perkins Hall from the moment he saw her, but issues from his past have left him guarded. Now that he has another chance with her, will he find the courage to share his life with her? Or will his emotional walls create a barrier that will leave him alone once more? Find out in this heartfelt, emotional third book (stand alone) in the Star Lake series.

The Heartbeats Series:

Where It All Began: Sandra Baker thought her life was on the right track until she ended up pregnant. Her boyfriend, not wanting the baby, pushes her to have an abortion. After the procedure, Sandra's life falls apart, and she turns to alcohol. Her relationship ends, and she struggles to find meaning in her life. When she meets Henry Dobbs, a strong Christian man, she begins to wonder if God would accept her. Will she tell Henry her darkest secret? And will she ever be able to forgive herself and find healing? Find out in this emotional love story.

The Power of Prayer: Callie Green thought she had her whole life planned out until her fiance left her at the altar. When her carefully laid plans crumble, she begins to make mistakes at work and engage in uncharacteristic activities. After a mistake nearly costs her her job, she cashes in her honeymoon tickets for some time away. There she meets JD, a charming Christian man who, even though she is not a believer, captures her interest. Before their relationship can deepen, Callie's ex-fiance shows back up in her life and she is forced to choose between Daniel and JD. Who will she choose and how will her choice affect the rest of her life? Find out in this touching novel.

When Hearts Collide: Amanda Adams has always been a Christian, but she's a novice at relationships. When she meets Caleb, her emotions get the best of her and she ignores the sign that something is amiss. Will she find out before it's too late? Jared Masterson is still healing from his girlfriend's strange rejection and disappearance when he meets Amanda. She captivates his heart, but can he save her from making the biggest mistake of her life? A must read for mothers and daughters. Though part of the series and the first of the college spin off series, it is a stand alone book and can be read separately.

A Past Forgiven: Jess Peterson has lived a life of abuse and lost her self worth, but when she is paired with a Christian roommate, she begins to wonder if there is a loving father looking down on her. Her decisions lead her one way, but when she ends up pregnant, she must make some major changes. Chad Michelson is healing from his own past and uses meaningless relationships to hide his pain, but when Jess becomes pregnant, he begins to wonder about the meaning of life. Can he step up and be there for Jess and the baby?

Sweet Billionaires Series:

The Billionaire's Secret: Maxwell Banks was the ultimate player until he found himself caring for a daughter he didn't know he had. Can he change to become the role model she needs? Alyssa Miller hasn't had the best luck with past relationships, so why is she falling for the one man who is sure to break her heart? Though nearly complete opposites, feelings develop, but can Max really change his philandering ways? Or will one mistake seal his fate forever?

A Brush with a Billionaire: Brent just wanted to finish his novel in peace, but when his car breaks down in Sweet Grove, he is forced to deal with a female mechanic and try to get along. Sam thought she had given up on city boys, but when Brent shows up in her shop, she finds herself fighting attraction. Will their stubborn natures keep them apart or can a small town festival bring them together?

The Billionaire's Christmas Miracle: Drew Devonshire is captivated by the woman he meets at a masquerade ball, but who is she? Gwen Rodgers is a teacher, but when she pretends to be her friend and meets Drew at a masquerade ball, her world gets thrown upside down.

The Billionaire's Cowboy Groom: Carrie Bliss finally found the man she wants to marry but there's just one little problem. She's technically still married. Cal Roper hasn't seen her in years but his heart still belongs to his wife. When she returns to town requesting a divorce, can he convince her they belong together?

The Cowboy Billionaire: Coming Soon!

The Lawkeeper Series:

Lawfully Matched: Kate Whidby doesn't want to impose on her newly married brother after their parents die, so she accepts a mail order bride offer in the paper. Little does she know the man she intends to marry has a dark past, sending her fleeing into a neighboring town and into Jesse Jenning's life. Jesse never wanted to be in law enforcement, but after a band of robbers kills his fiancee, he dons the badge and swears revenge. Will he find his fiancee's killer? And when Kate flies into his life, will he be able to put his painful past behind him in order to love again?

Lawfully Justified: William Cook turns to bounty hunting after losing his wife. When he suffers a life-threatening injury, he is forced to stay in town with an intriguing woman. Emma Stewart has moved back in with her widowed father, the town doctor, but she still longs for a family of her own, so no one is more surprised than she is when she starts to develop feeling for the bounty hunter, who hides his heart of gold behind a rugged exterior. Can Emma offer William a reason to stay? Can William find a way to heal from his broken past to start a future with Emma? Or will a haunting secret take away all the possibilities of this budding romance?

The Scarlet Wedding: William and Emma are planning their wedding, but an outbreak and a return from his past force them to change their plans. Is a happily ever after still in their future?

Lawfully Redeemed: Dani Higgins is a K9 cop looking to make a name for herself, but she finds herself at the mercy of a stranger after an accident. Calvin Phillips just wanted to help his brother, but somehow he ended up in the middle of a police investigation and caring for the woman trying to bring his brother in.

The Still Small Voice Series:

The Still Small Voice: Jordan Wright was searching for something after she gave her son up for adoption. What she found was God, and she began receiving visions. But can she trust Him when he asks her to do something big? Kat Jameson had long been a lukewarm Christian, but when her friend dies and she begins seeing lights, she thinks she is going crazy. Then she meets someone with a message for her. Will she be able to give up control and do what is asked of her?

A Spark in the Darkness coming soon!

Blushing Brides Series:

The Cowboy's Reality Bride: Tyler Hall just wanted to find love, but the women he dated wanted more than his small-town life provided. He gets more than he bargained for when he ends up on a reality dating show and falls for a woman who is not a contestant. Laney Swann has been running from her past for years, but it takes meeting a man on a reality dating show to make her see there's no need to run.

The Reality Bride's Baby: Laney wants nothing more than a baby, but when she starts feeling dizzy is it pregnancy or something more serious?

The Producer's Unlikely Bride: Justin Miller had given up on love, but when his image needs help, he finds himself needing the aid of a stranger who just happens to be a romance writer. Ava McDermott is waiting for the perfect love, but after agreeing to a fake relationship with Justin, she finds herself falling for real.

Ava's Blessing in Disguise: Five years after marriage, Ava faces a mysterious illness that threatens to ruin her career. Will she find out what it is?

The Soldier's Steadfast Bride: coming soon

The Men of Fire Beach

Fire Games: Cassidy returns home from Who Wants to Marry a Cowboy to find obsessive letters from a fan. The cop assigned to help her wants to get back to his case, but what she sees at a fire may just be the key he's looking for.

Lost Memories and New Beginnings: coming soon

Stand Alones:

Love Renewed: This books is part of the multi author second chance series. When fate reunites high school sweethearts separated by life's choices, can they find a second chance at love at a snowy lodge amid a little mystery?

Her children's early reader chapter book series:

The Wishing Stone #1: Dangerous Dinosaur
The Wishing Stone #2: Dragon Dilemma
The Wishing Stone #3: Mesmerizing Mermaids
The Wishing Stone #4: Pyramid Puzzle
The Wishing Stone Inspirations 1: Mary's Miracle
To see a list of all her books

authorloranahoopes.com
loranahoopes@gmail.com

ABOUT THE AUTHOR

Lorana Hoopes is an inspirational author originally from Texas but now living in the PNW with her husband and three children. When not writing, she can be seen kickboxing at the gym, singing, or acting on stage. One day, she hopes to retire from teaching and write full time.

Made in United States
Troutdale, OR
10/01/2023

13333481R00094